THE SECRET OF THE LOCH

THE SECRET OF THE LOCH

by

FRANCES COWEN

THE CHILDREN'S PRESS
LONDON AND GLASGOW

This Impression 1969

CONTENTS

CHAPTER ONE

THE GIRL FROM SCOTLAND

THE SUMMER TERM was almost at an end when Mary met—really met and got to know—Katrine Maclure.

Mary was one of those girls, frank and outspoken, who could not keep anything to herself, especially if it were good and exciting news.

The good and exciting news came a week before the end of term in a long letter from her mother. It was so exciting that when the post came, although she was due for class, she read it quickly, eyes glowing, and exclaimed to a friend who, with half a dozen other Fourth Formers, should have been on their way to gym: "How absolutely wizard!"

"What is it?" asked Betty Daines, casting a prefectorial eye on the others.

"Marvellous news. You know we live in London? Oh, it isn't so bad really, a flat in an old house in an old square. But now Mummy and Lilian have taken a house in Scotland. Listen: '*it's deep in the moors and overlooks a loch and we should do really well there*'."

"Do well?"

Mary nodded. "It's going to be a guest house, and it's called . . . wait a minute . . . The Old Manse. Betty, it's almost too good to be true. The boys will be able to fish and swim and run wild—it will be a real holiday, and I can make myself useful."

"It sounds super for you. London's no fun in the summer—well not much." Betty rather liked London, but her experience of it was confined to going up for the day to do a show or to shop.

"It can be a bit grim," confessed Mary, "with Mummy going to the office every day and Jim and Andrew getting restless."

The second bell rang. Betty, who understood a little, gave her friend's arm a squeeze and they both hurried off.

Mary had the part of Puck in a drastically cut version of *A Midsummer Night's Dream*, the end-of-term play which was to be performed in the school grounds. In spite of this, and the tennis finals, not to mention the last papers of the terminal exams, the wonderful news coloured Mary's busy days.

It meant so much to them all, as well she knew, for their mother had had something of a struggle to manage. Their father, a Naval Officer, had, after surviving the war, died very suddenly of some obscure disease contracted out east, when Mary was six, and her brothers seven and four respectively. Mrs. Carew had lived on her pension until the children could go to school and then had taken a secretarial post to help out. Luckily Mary had managed to get a scholarship to this famous school where she worked hard and played hard, looking forward to the time when she would be eighteen and ready to find some good post. Mother's news had been quite out of the blue. Lilian, whom they called Aunt Lilian was not an aunt at all, but their mother's best friend, herself a widow and childless. Now it seemed that an unexpected legacy had enabled her to buy this house in Scotland, for she herself was a Scot.

"Of course I haven't seen the place, but Lilian knows it well, as she once lived in the district. I gather it's a bit shabby, but there are eight bedrooms, and in the summer, right into October, we should manage to let well, for although it is rather isolated, two miles from the village and fifteen from Perth, the nearest big town, it is quite a beauty spot, and not far from the old castle of Lendaloch."

So wrote her mother. Mary reread that letter more than once, and her own little circle of friends were happy and pleased for her. Soon the news filtered round the school:

"Mary Carew's so excited. She's going to live in Scotland."

And, because Mary was very well liked, everybody was delighted, in so far as their own pre-holiday affairs allowed them to be.

There were about twenty scholarship girls at Holdean Manor School; the large number of paying scholars took life, on the whole, more easily. And the girls from wealthy families were easily identified by their sporting equipment, from tennis rackets to hockey sticks, the cut of their clothes, and the fine cars which arrived to take them out on high days and holidays.

There may have been a little envy here and there, but Mary had no envy in her. Some people had more of the world's goods than others. Why worry? She meant to succeed and help the family as soon as she left school. All the same, most of her own friends were from the scholarship faction.

That was why she looked up in some surprise when, one afternoon of the last week in term as she lay on the turf watching the tennis finals, Katrine Maclure, tall in well-cut tennis shorts and monogrammed shirt, came and joined her. Katrine was a dark, handsome girl, a little older than Mary. She was a senior prefect, and would be Head Girl next term.

As Mary looked at the clear-cut face, she saw that the girl was pale under her tan, her blue eyes darkly pooled, and she remembered that Katrine had had some bad news about her father recently. He had been killed in an accident—such had been the rumour, but she had not heard the particulars as she did not know Katrine or her set at all well.

"Hallo, Mary," was the other girl's greeting, "looking forward to the holidays?"

"Yes, rather." Mary hesitated but did not enlarge on her wonderful news.

Katrine looked at her round face, the bright hair cut short, and smiled; she, too, hesitated a moment then asked quickly, "Is it true that you've taken a house in Scotland?"

"Yes. It's wonderful, I can scarcely wait."

"I did hear that it was near Lendaloch."

"Yes, it is. I looked it up on the map but it wasn't shown. I suppose it's quite a small place. Do you know it?"

"I know Lendaloch." Katrine spoke soberly.

"It's beautiful, isn't it? Do tell me about it."

"Well, the loch is very deep, with trees coming down to it on one side, and to the east there's rock on the shores and the moors roll away, purple and misty, to Benavar, the mountain," she spoke dreamily, remembering.

"We've taken the Old Manse," Mary told her.

"I know it, of course. It's three miles from the castle round the loch. You'll see the castle from your windows —the old part, that is—a great tower which dates back to the twelfth century."

"It sounds marvellous."

"I do hope they're keeping up the garden. Perhaps they'll let it."

Mary was puzzled and looked it.

Katrine shook back her dark hair. "How stupid I am. I was talking of the castle. I live there, you know."

"At Lendaloch! I knew you were Scottish but I had no idea . . ."

"It's true, but now Father's gone . . ." her mouth trembled. Mary was acutely embarrassed. "I say, I am sorry. . . ."

Suddenly the older girl began to speak quickly. "Listen! Aunt Enid, she's almost my only relative, wants me to go on a cruise with her at the end of August, but first I'm to stay with her in Hampstead. Mary, would you do something for me?"

"Of course, if I can."

"I heard that your people were going to let rooms in the Old Manse, take guests. Could I be one, one of your first?"

She spoke urgently, as if it were terribly important to her. Touched and still bewildered, Mary began to explain.

"Yes, we are, and you could, of course. You see Mummy and a friend are running it together, this friend's bought it. There are lots of bedrooms and, as it's quite a beauty spot, we hope it will succeed."

"Could I come, as a guest then, soon?"

"I'm sure you can. Mummy will be delighted. You might even be our first guest, as you say."

Katrine stared, frowning at a hard-fought game of singles. "I'm afraid I'll have to say you've invited me. But I'll be a guest of course." She flushed.

"Shall I ask Mother to write to you then?"

"Could you, then I'll show it to my aunt? Your mother could say that you've asked me and can I come."

"I'll do that to-day then."

"That's sweet of you." Katrine frowned, "I don't want you to think I'm underhand, but I'd rather Auntie didn't know exactly where it is until—until I get there."

"But why not?"

"I've a good reason. I really have. She might not want me to go to the castle."

"No? But it's your home." Mary stopped. "Oh, of course as there's no one there, you'd like to stay with us and go to it now and then to look round?"

Katrine laughed; she sounded relieved.

"That's about the way of it. You'll think I'm an idiot." Suddenly she went sober again. "I must go there. I must. It's terribly important for me, Mary."

Mary found nothing to say.

"You do understand?"

"Of course I do." This was not strictly true. She had not understood Katrine's nervousness, her varying changes of mood, and her reference to her father who had "gone".

Some of Katrine's friends came racing up at this moment. As Katrine got up, she said, "You will write to your mother to-day, and ask her to ask me? Promise?"

"I promise."

Once alone, Mary went off to change, thoughtfully. Until to-day she had scarcely exchanged two words with the Scottish girl. Why had she been so intense—so mysterious—about the proposed visit? Perhaps she had guessed that Mary's family were not well-off and had been embarrassed at asking herself as a guest. Not that Mother would mind her having a friend to stay but Katrine was not, strictly speaking, a friend. And what had happened to her father?

Finding Betty in the common-room before tea she asked her as casually as she could.

"Betty, I've been talking to Katrine Maclure. Did you know she lives at Lendaloch, where we're going?"

"No, I didn't. Funny about her father," Betty replied.

"What happened?"

"Someone told me it was in the papers. He disappeared

about three weeks ago, and as far as I know he hasn't been found."

"Disappeared? But how?"

"I told you I don't know exactly what happened. I know the seniors were talking about it, but not much because it's so awful for Katrine. Why do you ask, Mary?"

"I was chatting to her as I told you. I like her."

"Oh, she's very sound," said Betty after the manner of her undergraduate brother.

Well, she knew just a little more, and that little made her feel really sorry for Katrine. Being a practical girl, she kept her promise and wrote to her mother, saying that one of the girls would like to come and stay and would she please write to Miss Katrine Maclure at the school and invite her.

"She lives, it seems, at the Castle of Lendaloch but it is closed at present. She's awfully keen to come and I'm sure you'll like her."

She caught the post that evening for she knew that her mother was leaving their flat at the beginning of next week and that she would be very busy packing. But she could rely on her mother to write off in time.

After prayers that night Katrine hurried up to her.

"Have you written?" she asked.

"Yes, I put it down to be collected before six. It should have gone by now."

"You're an angel, thanks."

During the next few rather hectic days which marked the end of term, in spite of the play, in spite of the chatter, and preparations and planning for the long holidays, Katrine managed to have more than one talk with Mary.

She would leave her own friends and seek Mary out, and, when she did so, she talked of Lendaloch, eyes bright and rather wistful.

She mentioned her father, but Mary never got up enough courage to ask her definitely what had happened to him.

"Daddy and I were going to spend the whole summer there this year," she said once. "We were going to fish, and later there was to be a house-party for the shooting. He had planned to buy a motor-launch."

Mary waited; then, to break the silence said inanely, "How lovely."

"Yes." The other changed the subject quickly in a way she had. "You'll love the manse of course. Now tell me about yourself. You have brothers?"

"Two. Jim, who is seventeen, and Andrew only thirteen. They're both at boarding-school. They break up this week, too. I expect they're awfully excited about going to Scotland."

Katrine let her talk about them, saying little after that, listening, but her thoughts seemed far away . . . in Scotland no doubt.

Mrs. Carew wrote to Katrine within a couple of days. It was a short hurried note telling Katrine that she would be very welcome in their new home; and, apparently, just what Katrine wanted.

"I can show Aunt Enid this. In fact I'll send it on to her. There's no reason really why we shouldn't travel up together."

"Don't you want to see your aunt?"

Katrine shrugged. "She's a dear, she lectures on economics at London University, but she's so busy she hasn't much time for me. She won't mind."

Mary felt sorry. Poor Katrine, had she no one who really cared how and where she spent her holidays, whether she came or went? She thought of her own family, of her mother who cared for and worried about them all, and realised that, in her own way, she was luckier than this girl with all her money and a castle to call her own.

It was on the eve of the general exodus from the big school, with discipline relaxed, and even the mistresses unbending and talking with their pupils during the apology for classes, that Katrine came up and took her arm.

"Let's stroll in the garden," she said, "I'd like a chat."

So they strolled out into the grounds, past the piles of luggage already mounting in the hall and round the playing fields.

"I heard from my aunt to-day. It's O.K. As a matter of fact, I think she's glad. There's a conference at Oxford she wants to attend in August."

"So you'll travel up with us?"

"Yes. She sent me thirty quid, that should do fares and everything."

Mary remembered with wry amusement the five pounds for her expenses received that morning. Evidently the larger sum meant little or nothing to Katrine; probably because she had never had to consider money at all.

"I'm so glad you're coming," she said. "It's a long journey, the longest I've ever been on."

"I'm glad, too. But I'm pretty used to travelling. Daddy took me to Rome for the Olympics the other year, and last year we went to the United States."

"Ooh! Did you like it?"

"It was all right."

The night was heavy, the sky overcast, with thunder rolling somewhere over the Sussex Downs.

"We get big storms over the loch sometimes," commented Katrine, "then everything goes black and the thunder reverberates over Benavar. When I was little I used to get frightened. Old Jeannie told me the legend and I would think of it; Daddy was very annoyed with her about that."

"Is there a legend about the castle?"

"Yes. Lots of those old Scottish places have their own legends. Like Glamis."

"Glamis? Oh of course, where Princess Margaret was born. Isn't there a secret room there, and a secret too which only the eldest son is allowed to know?"

"Something like that."

"Do tell me. Your legend, I mean."

"The legend of Lendaloch? Sounds good, doesn't it?"

"It sounds exciting."

Katrine paused by the ramp above the playing fields. From the big, grey mansion which was the school came the sound of the younger girls having a sing-song.

> "*Oh I went down south for to see my Sal,*
> *Sing Polly-wolly-doodle all the day . . .*"

Mary was to remember that old Negro song long after as a background to something quite incongruous to it: the legend of Lendaloch as told by Katrine.

"It's a funny old tale," she began, "the kind of story that grows like a snowball as it's passed on from one generation to the other. It begins with the Wee Folk as they call them in the Highlands."

"Fairies, yes, go on."

"Fairies, if you like. Well a tribe of the Wee Folk lived in a glen far inland, surrounded by wooded mountains. It was said to be heavenly there, an earthly paradise, but it had a bad reputation because if anyone wandered there by chance, they were never seen again."

"Like ' The Island that Liked to be Visited,'" quoted Mary.

"You mean Barrie's play, *Mary Rose*? Well, something like that, I suppose. Anyway, a chieftain who had lost a man in the glen, rallied a party to raid it. It took them some time to locate it but, when they did, it was very beautiful, just as beautiful as the stories had made it, full of flowers they could not name, and tropical fruit. Led by the chieftain they tore down the flowers and vines in revenge, and they were doing this, when there was a loud roar of rushing waters and a tiny burn which had run through the glen, widened and became a churning flood which filled the place before they could escape."

"What a story!"

"Yes, but listen to the rest." Katrine glanced at the green of the playing-fields, and the house, now casting a long shadow. "Years after this a great Scottish family were to live above this very place—our family."

"But what happened after the drowning of all those people?"

"Sorry, I'm telling the story badly. Well, one man survived; the young son of the chieftain, and he built himself a hut and stayed there on the verge of the drowned glen. Some say that he became a magician and saw the future in the loch itself, others that he had an enchanted mirror which showed him what was to come. It's all rather vague, you see."

"But thrilling."

"Perhaps. When our family came years and years after, they built the castle on the edge of the loch where the chieftain's son had lived; it's even said that they were the descendants of the tribe who had ruined the glen and been drowned. Anyhow part of the old castle, the tower still stands, and, the weird part of the whole thing is that one member of the family, often the heir, disappears in every third generation."

Mary stiffened. The juniors were still singing, and in the far distance summer lightning rent the sky.

"In the Castle of Lendaloch?"

"Yes. I'm telling you the legend for what it's worth." Katrine spoke crisply. "One in every third generation. There's supposed to be a secret room in the tower, the Room of the Mirror, it's called. In a funny sort of way it's all linked up with the old story of the Wee Folk and their ruined glen and the magician, so-called."

"What is there in the Room of the Mirror then?" asked Mary.

"That's where they're supposed to meet their fate."

"But surely it isn't true?"

Katrine shook her head. "Not all of it, naturally."

"But do people really disappear?"

The other girl nodded. "Yes, it's in the old records. Richard in the time of the Wars of the Roses, James who fought for Charles the First, another James in Queen Anne's day. Then my great-grandfather was drowned in the loch, we think, his body was never found. Now, of course . . ."

Mary felt a little cold as she looked at the other girl's face which had gone white and still.

"Now? What do you mean?"

"Three weeks ago my father disappeared. He was staying at the castle, I'd had a letter from him the day before, then—well, he just vanished. They searched the moors, tried to drag the loch. Now you know why I want to go back there."

For a moment Mary could not speak.

"They haven't found any trace of him?"

"No. He could swim like a champion, he was most awfully strong and well, and he knew the countryside like the back of his hand, but he's gone."

"And you think it's the kind of family curse?"

"Not really, no. Oh, sometimes I do, but no, not really. I don't see how it could be, but you see why I want to go there."

"But surely the police have done everything they can?"

"I suppose so," Katrine spoke dully.

"And you're alone now?"

"I am," she smiled sadly, "the Maclure of the Maclures, though I'm not so sure that they would call me The Maclure like—like they did Daddy. Yes, I'm pretty well alone. We've got some cousins overseas, in New Zealand as a matter of fact, but we rarely hear from them. My mother died when I was a baby so I am left alone," she spoke almost proudly as though defying pity.

Mary caught her arm. "Well, you won't be alone with us at the Manse anyhow."

"I know, that's why I was so interested when I heard about you taking the old place."

"All the same I can well understand that your aunt might not want you to go back to Lendaloch."

"I must go back."

Looking at her, Mary felt even a little afraid. If her father had disappeared like this, met perhaps with some fatal accident not yet discovered, it was the last place she should go to. All the same she knew that it was no good voicing these opinions to Katrine.

They had made the circuit of the playing-fields and were turning round towards the big main drive.

"Let's hurry," said Katrine, "we're going to miss the bell."

As they reached the drive itself a man, who seemed to have been standing by the lodge, turned quickly and walked away.

Mary thought little of it: just a curious passer-by interested in the well-known school, that was all, but Katrine held her arm almost fiercely.

"Did you see him?" she asked in a tight, tense voice.

"That man? Yes, just curious, I suppose."

"I've seen him before, more than once. Mary, I think he's watching me."

Mary almost recoiled; for a moment she began to think that Katrine's imagination, affected by her father's disappearance and an old legend heard in childhood, had unbalanced her mind.

"Why should he? Katrine, you mustn't imagine things."

"I don't, that's the trouble. I've seen him before; for the last week he's been wandering round here, and he watches me, I know that." She stopped, noticing Mary's expression. "Forget it. Perhaps it is my imagination."

They walked swiftly on to the school.

A bell sounded in the evening silence. The juniors had finished their sing-song, but there was still a rumble of thunder from the north.

"Supper," said Mary with forced cheerfulness, "and let's look forward to the holidays. After all, you'll be all right with us at the Manse."

Katrine smiled.

"Who said I wouldn't?" she asked.

CHAPTER TWO

OVER THE BORDER

PERHAPS BECAUSE her mother was so busy, Mary had not received any final directions about the journey to Lendaloch. Certainly Mrs. Carew had sent her some money and said that she had written to Jim and Andrew at their school, but, after an abortive search in an old time-table in the library, she was still wondering about times and trains when the morrow dawned, wondering almost whether she had not dreamed up the whole thing.

Still Katrine would be with her, and Katrine was familiar with the journey and used to travelling.

However, there was a letter from her brother Jim that morning. He and Andrew had officially broken up the day before but stayed overnight at the school.

"I've made inquiries and there's a train direct to Perth from Euston at nine-fifty. So you can meet us at Victoria at nine. We'll cross London and get to Euston in good time. We'd better get some fodder as I heard from one of the characters in my form that it costs the earth to lunch on the train, and you know what Andrew is for his food. I must say, old girl, that it's great news about the house. Anyhow, see you to-morrow and don't be late for goodness' sake."

The school buses were already lining up. Luckily Mary had packed the night before, but she rushed off to find Katrine and tell her the news.

Katrine was in her own little room, talking to matron when Mary burst in.

"We've got to get the eight-fifteen, Katrine," she said.

"Jim and Andrew are meeting us at Victoria at nine, and we're going straight over to Euston."

"All right, don't get so het up." Katrine laughed, then added: "I'd no idea we were travelling up with your brothers."

"Why not?"

"The more the merrier, though I rather hoped we'd fly to Edinburgh then take the train on to Perth."

It wasn't a bit of use telling Katrine that flying was distinctly more expensive than the train journey, so Mary merely fidgeted, looking at the half-opened case.

Katrine noticed her glance and calmly closed and clicked it to. "There. Two cases should do me. I can always buy anything I want in Perth, if necessary."

Matron smiled at Mary.

"Aren't you a lucky girl to be going to Scotland," she said. "It's lovely at this time of year. But then you are Scottish, Katrine?"

Katrine nodded soberly, and Mary remembered that uncanny story she had heard from her only last night. In fact she had lain awake some time thinking of it before she slept. Still she had no time for any such brooding now.

Katrine was annoyingly calm, eating her breakfast without even a glance at the clock; Mary hurriedly gobbled hers and, when they finally caught one of the school buses and were driven swiftly along the cliffs to Brighton, she at least felt as though she had been running a race.

Katrine got into a compartment with a trio of her friends and Mary was a little out of it, although the older girl brought her into the conversation pleasantly enough.

"I'm spending the beginning of the holiday with Mary in Scotland," she explained.

The others stared in some surprise, then went on

discussing their own plans. Mary at least was glad when the express got in at Victoria.

It was Katrine who calmly engaged a porter; Katrine, wearing a light coat over a summer frock, looked, to Mary, who still wore her school uniform, quite grown up.

As they walked towards the barrier she suddenly remembered that the boys didn't know about their guest.

Then she saw Jim's tall figure standing at the barrier and, as usual, she glowed. Jim was inclined to take advantage of his status as head of the family, but she adored him in spite of that. And as for Andrew, who was broad-set and fair, in features at least very like her, the two of them had always been very close.

Once through the barrier she hurried up to them.

Jim looked her up and down. "On time. Wonders will never cease!" he remarked. "Andrew's hungry, let's go and have some chow."

Andrew grabbed her arm. "I've got a fishing-rod, Mary; swopped it with a chap for my stamp collection."

"Andrew! And I'd been saving some for you."

"Never mind, I'll start again in the winter."

Katrine, who had been talking to a porter, came up and surveyed the two boys pleasantly.

"I hate train meals, Mary, so I've told the porter to get a taxi. We'll call in at Fortnum and Masons for a hamper."

Jim's good-looking face showed surprise quickly hidden and Andrew just goggled.

Katrine held out her hand to Jim.

"I'm Katrine Maclure. I can see that Mary hasn't even told you I'm coming up with you."

"N-no. How do you do."

He gave Mary a reproachful glance.

"I'm sorry I didn't, but you scarcely ever write. Mother knows though. Katrine used to live at the castle."

Jim raised his dark brows as he turned to Katrine. "I say, is that true? Always thought of people who live in Scottish castles as kilted and hefty with the whale of a Scottish accent. Not that I don't like it," he added kindly.

"That's good to know anyhow," Katrine replied with faint sarcasm.

Jim glanced at the clock, it was already ten-past nine. "I suggest we get going."

"I've got a taxi," Katrine spoke over her shoulder as she led the way.

Glancing from her brother to her new friend, Mary hoped that they would eventually get on together. At seventeen, Jim rather felt his superiority.

Unfortunately, when the taxi took them up to Piccadilly he was rather inclined to argue. Katrine took no notice but hurried into the big shop leaving them in the cab, and returned in a creditably short time with a man carrying an outsize hamper.

It was balanced by the driver, they were saluted, and were about to drive away when Katrine, who was just getting in, was stopped by a passer-by.

He was a tall, middle-aged man, wearing well-cut tweeds and a Robin-Hood hat on the side of his head.

"Katrine, my dear, by all that's wonderful. Where are you off to?"

"I'm going on holiday with some friends."

"But of course. And where?"

Katrine gave him a quick look. "Scotland."

"Now Katrine . . ."

But she was already inside the taxi and slammed the door. "Sorry, Sir Henry, due at Euston any minute now."

The cab drove off leaving him staring after them.

Katrine sat back, her cheeks a little flushed, and sighed.

"Who was that?" asked Andrew.

"A friend of my father's."

"Why didn't he want you to go to Scotland?"

"Be quiet," said his sister. "He *will* always ask questions," she told Katrine.

But Andrew had been right—the man whom Katrine had addressed as "Sir Henry" had been even a little alarmed when she had mentioned her destination.

All Katrine said was, "That's the worst of the West End, one's always running into people."

"Ha-ha!" Jim chortled wickedly.

Katrine ignored him.

The train was not overcrowded and they got into one of those wide carriages with little tables between the seats which make a long journey so much easier in case one wants to play cards, or any other game for that matter.

They sat opposite each other, the two girls and the two boys, and Jim remarked with wicked pleasure that they would be about ten hours on the train.

"Are you sure?" Katrine sounded appalled. "We usually fly up to Edinburgh, flying is so much quicker," she added.

"You're telling me! Well, we get to Perth at seven-forty. I've written Mother and she'll expect us about nine."

"To think that we got to New York in five hours last year," remarked Katrine. "Air travel does save so much time."

"You've been to the States then?" asked Andrew.

"Yes."

"What was it like? Did you see the Empire State Building and the U.N.O. box-thing at Lake Success and . . ."

Mary sat and looked out of the window as the train began to shake London from its wheels, and let Andrew go on asking questions. Ten hours! Almost a day! Jim got out a map he had bought and began to show her the way they were going. "Right up England, through Carlisle to Carstairs. A lovely, long journey!"

Katrine, who had satisfied, for the time, Andrew's interest in the United States, said nothing. She had bought some magazines and began to read them, isolating herself, as it were, from their family circle.

The family had a lot to discuss.

"I could scarcely believe it when Mother gave me the gen about this venture of hers and Aunt Lil's," said Jim. "I only hope it turns out all right."

"It will," Mary assured him, "it must. It's a beautiful place and Aunt Lilian's already advertised it. A guest-house at Lendaloch, think of it!"

"I hope it isn't too much for Mother." Jim spoke thoughtfully, his tones scarcely audible above the roar of the train. "Anyhow, we can put our backs into it. Hew wood and draw water."

"And catch fish in the loch," added Andrew.

"I think Mother will love it. She didn't really like her job at the office, day after day with only about three weeks' holiday a year. I thought she looked pretty rotten at Easter."

"I know. Oh, I'm glad for her, Mary. As a matter of fact I noticed it too, how ill she looked, I mean, and I've almost decided to go into business when I leave school."

"No, Jim, you know you want to be a doctor."

"And spend another six years working for it? I'm not all that sure."

"Mother would be the first to hate the idea," Mary sighed. "I wish we had tons of money like some people."

She broke off quickly as Katrine rustled her magazine, and flushed.

"I'm going to have tons of money. I'm going to have a garage and sell cars," Andrew said.

On and on rushed the train and the discussion continued. Each of them had their own ideas about the Old Manse.

"I expect it's a great red-brick place in a rambling garden with huge rooms and a massive kitchen," surmised Jim, probably thinking of a rectory he had visited when staying with friends.

"I imagine it as low and rambling, with creepers on the walls, and a garden, of course, and a little stream running through it, only in Scotland they'd call it a burn," said Mary.

"You're both wrong you know," Katrine had looked up from her reading. "It's a dear old place, and it's built of grey stone, granite from Aberdeen, it's got a lovely garden in front, by the winding road, and a small terrace off the two big living-rooms from which you can see the loch through the trees. Behind is the kitchen garden, below the spruce fir woods, and on a fine day Benavar shows purple-tipped beyond."

Jim stared. "You know it then?"

"Oh, yes. Old Colonel Burton, who was a friend of my father's, lived there before he died. I knew it was to be sold."

"I say. Then you'll be able to show us round?"

"Of course. Lendaloch, that's the village, is five miles from it though, but there are some quite good shops there for groceries and things. We used to drive into Perth for real shopping." She paused, "Luckily there is a telephone."

Jim's dark brown eyes were studying Katrine with interest.

"How come you're staying with us and not at the castle?"

Katrine went cold and tense again.

"Because the castle is closed now. I can't very well go and live there on my own."

"Oh, no, rather not."

He was still obviously puzzled and Mary regretted that she had not taken the opportunity of telling her brother all about Katrine when they had waited in the taxi in Piccadilly. But Katrine had been very quick getting the hamper and there had not really been time.

As it was the girl had now given them a clearer picture of their new home and they went on discussing everything with growing anticipation.

"A vegetable garden," said Andrew, "I love gardening; probably we can grow all our own vegetables and fruit." He looked across at Katrine, "Are there raspberries?"

"Raspberries?"

"Yes, in the garden of The Old Manse?"

"I don't really know. But there is a small orchard, apple and pear trees, and Colonel Burton used to grow peaches on a south wall."

"Yum-yum."

Mary watched her younger brother with amusement, he certainly had a healthy interest in food.

The train was forging its way through the Midlands, past the Potteries, when they began to think of food.

Jim got down the hamper, and Katrine, with a mischievous little glance at Andrew, began to unpack it.

They all stared at the contents. There were four small cooked chickens, individual salads, biscuits, cheese crisps and a game pie, jellies and figs and a large box of chocolates.

"Perhaps we could put this aside for your mother if she likes chocolates," said Katrine thoughtfully.

None of the Carews had seen such a spread.

"My word, you have certainly done us proud," said Jim.

Katrine smiled and said in her rather old-fashioned way, "Let's say it's my contribution to the journey."

When a waiter came through calling that first luncheons were being served, they looked at other people going to the dining-car almost pityingly.

The meal over, the two girls left the compartment and moved along the speeding train to wash.

On their way they had to pass through another carriage and Mary noticed that Katrine, glancing at someone, hurried on rather quickly.

As they returned she put her hand on Mary's arm. "Let's stand here a bit and look out," she said, "I want to talk to you."

They stood and stared at the flying countryside.

Katrine began to speak quickly.

"Listen, Mary, I shall have to leave this train, at Carlisle I think."

"What on earth are you talking about?"

"Never mind. There's someone on it who knows me. I'm almost sure I'm being followed."

"But why? Katrine, you're imagining things again."

"Very well. I shall go on ahead of you. We pass through a carriage like ours, with not many people—there are a lot at lunch. There's a man there with a red face, wearing a tatty sort of suit under a raincoat. Mary, he's the man we saw at Holdean, hanging around the grounds. You *must* remember."

"But Katrine, are you sure you're not mistaken?"

"I'm sure. Just you look."

Not really knowing what to think, Mary followed Katrine, who strode between the aisles of that compartment, head very erect, looking at nobody.

Mary might not have seen the man for he sat with his back to them, playing patience, carefully putting down card after card, but as Katrine passed, he paused and looked up, and his glance followed her as she went through and out.

Mary hesitated near him, pretending to look in her handbag. He had a reddish face, a rather tatty tweed suit, he wore no hat, and she noticed the dark hair receding from a narrow forehead above a narrow, rather rat-like face. It could be the man they had seen in the grounds of the school; in fact she was almost sure it was, and yet wasn't Katrine letting her imagination run away with her, and allowing a passing likeness to convince her?

She reached her seat to find the two boys playing some complicated card game of their own. Katrine stood and faced her.

"Well?"

"It did look like him, but I'm not absolutely sure."

Katrine nodded soberly. "But I am. I'm being followed. He mustn't know where I'm going so I shall get off the train at Carlisle and take another later on to you. I'll leave my luggage, and just take my bag."

"But, Katrine . . ."

Jim had noticed that they were arguing, although he could not have heard what they were saying above the roar of the train.

"Hey you two, something up?"

Katrine sat down and smiled easily at him.

"What should be the matter? What's that game you're playing and where did you get the cards?"

"Brought 'em with us. Knew it was a long journey."

"Let's all play then."

So they played whist, at Andrew's request, and the train rumbled on to Crewe, stopped, then continued on its way.

Mary wished that she could talk things over with Katrine. Sooner or later she would have to tell her brothers, or at least Jim, the odd situation in which her new friend seemed to be involved. Odd? It was really rather frightening.

She watched the cards, trumped Jim's ace, and went on playing very badly.

They were beginning to climb between the rugged moors west of the Pennines and approaching Cumberland, when Katrine sat back and gave Mary a quick look.

"I'm going out for a wash in a moment, come with me, Mary."

Mary glanced at her watch, they must be nearing Carlisle.

A few minutes later and they were again moving through the next compartment. The man still sat playing his eternal game of patience, another traveller now sat next to him and seemed to be advising him about the cards.

The thin face was bent, and he did not look up as they passed.

Katrine walked on through the swaying train, then stood between the carriages much farther up.

"Now, we're coming into Carlisle in about ten minutes," she said. "I shall get off. Don't return to your compartment until the train has gone on again."

"But Katrine, must you? I don't like it."

"I must. I can't take any risks. No one must know I'm going to Lendaloch, least of all this man."

"Do you know who he is then?"

"No, I don't. I don't understand a great deal. But I'm going to find out when I get to your place."

"But will you be all right?"

Katrine laughed wryly. "I'm used to travelling, I'll come over to you by easy stages. I can get a car from

Perth, I imagine. So expect me any time after ten to-night."

Mary caught the other's arm. "Do be careful, Katrine."

"I'll be careful all right."

The train was slowing down. It began to enter the city, and soon stopped. Katrine looked into her bag, then smiled.

"'Bye for the present, Mary. And I'll be all right." She paused, "You can tell Jim a bit about this, have to, I suppose, but you will wait, won't you?"

She nodded, smiled, and hurried down a corridor. The train seemed to wait for an interminable time at the station, and Mary stood where she was, staring out. There was no sign of Katrine on the platform. At last they crawled out and began to get up speed again.

Mary found her way back to their own carriage. She dared not glance at the man who had scared Katrine off the train, but he was there, and she felt rather than saw him look up and stare as she walked on and through the compartment.

The boys had stopped playing and both looked up when they saw her.

"Something wrong?" queried Jim. "Train sick?"

"No, Jim, you know I never am."

"Katrine is then?"

"Katrine's left the train."

Both Jim and Andrew stared, Andrew open mouthed. "Left the train? What *is* all this?"

Mary sank down opposite them and tried to find words, the right convincing words, to tell them all she knew about Katrine and her strange quest at Lendaloch.

CHAPTER THREE

THE OLD MANSE

THE BOYS listened with incredulity, such incredulity that Mary did not touch on the legend; that, she felt, might make them doubt the tale altogether.

Finally Jim asked a few pertinent questions. "Katrine told you that her father has disappeared. Did she say how?"

"No. It was three weeks ago. It was even in the papers, so I heard. She said they searched for him on the moors, dragged the loch and everything. That's all."

"Sounds bad. If he were still alive surely he'd have got in touch with her. What can she do when she does get to Lendaloch? The police must have covered every possibility."

"I know. Though, in a way, I can understand her wanting to go there."

"And now this business about someone following her. Why should anyone do that? What is he like by the way?"

"Very ordinary looking."

"Are you sure he was the man you saw near the school?"

"I only had a glimpse of him."

Andrew, silent because his quick mind had formed so many questions, suddenly got up. "Where is he? I'd like a glimpse at him."

"The third carriage down, facing the engine on the left. He seems to have been playing patience the entire journey."

Jim got up also. "Wait, we'll both go," he decided. Doubtfully, Mary watched them sidle out of the swaying carriage. However, they were back in a surprisingly short time.

Andrew threw himself down.

"No such person," he said.

Jim nodded. "No man playing patience. You'd better go and look, Mary."

Heart sinking, for this might mean that Katrine was right and that her ruse in leaving the train had been discovered, Mary went out and along the train.

That they were now in Scotland, that the very countryside had already begun to show the wild moors, purple tipped, that within less than two hours they would be in Perth, did not seem to matter. Although she usually sat watching the flying landscape when travelling, they had travelled the length of England and she had scarcely noticed a landmark.

She reached the carriage, the same passengers were there, some now sleeping, others reading, but no man with a narrow rat-like face in shabby tweeds sat there now. She turned and went back to the boys.

"He's gone?" asked Jim.

She nodded. "Jim, I'm frightened. He must have guessed that Katrine was leaving the train. And she's all alone, too."

"Don't panic." Jim was reassuring. "How could he know?"

"Look here," Andrew leaned forward, "why should she be followed? I mean she hasn't got the plans of a secret invention or anything like that?"

Mary had to laugh. "You read too many spy stories. No, but it is odd that her father disappeared like that, and now she's going up to Lendaloch. Couldn't it be someone who knows what happened to her father?"

Jim shook his head. "Sounds a bit far-fetched to me."
Mary was tempted, and fell.

"Of course I haven't told you the legend," she said.

Andrew stared. "What legend?"

"Oh, it's very old, but people disappear in every third generation."

"You mean people of the Maclure family?"

"Yes. She told me. It's a sort of tradition in the family, which makes her father's disappearance, well, kind of worse."

Jim was frowning.

"What is the legend?"

So she told him the old story which Katrine had told her some three days ago: about the ravaging of the valley by the chieftain and the clan, about his return to live by the verge of the loch and the secret mirror which might or might not be the glassy face of the loch itself.

Her brothers listened with commendable patience, then Jim shook his head.

"Poor kid, no wonder she's nervy. But I don't like it."

"What do you mean, Jim?"

"I don't quite know!" His dark eyes were thoughtful. "Oh, I don't believe in the legend, that's just a legend, but, don't you see, it might give ideas to people who know about it."

"What ideas?"

"Well, she's alone now. Someone might be trying to frighten her; they might even want to get her out of the way. Has she any relations?"

"An aunt in London. I don't know really. The aunt sounds all right. She lectures at London University."

"I say," Andrew looked really excited, "do you think she's in danger then?"

"I don't know," Jim frowned. "Anyhow if she gets to us all right, we'll darned well keep an eye on her."

"If?" Mary whitened, thinking of Katrine on her own.

"Don't look so frightened. She struck me as quite an intelligent girl, and she's obviously used to travelling. She'll turn up, I expect." He stopped.

Someone, the sound of his approach silenced in the roar of a passing train on the down line, stood by their table.

"Excuse me, my watch has stopped. Any of you got the time?" The voice was clear and a little sharp.

Mary stared at pale eyes, close-set under a domed forehead, the dark hair receding. She swallowed and looked away as Jim glanced at his wrist-watch and gave the time.

"Almost on seven," he said.

"Good. Perth in forty minutes."

He nodded, smiled slightly, and went on.

Mary sat back: relief on her face.

"What on earth's the matter?" Jim stared at her.

"That was he, the man Katrine thought was following her."

Jim laughed. "You see? Really, old girl, I do begin to think that it's all a lot of nonsense. That poor kid is all het up and no wonder—her father has vanished and she's been fed with eerie legends since she was knee-high to a buttercup. Now all we have to do is to keep an eye on her and see that she doesn't do anything foolish."

"I do hope you're right." Mary spoke faintly but without conviction. Still, she relaxed and began to stare out at the country whilst Andrew, all but forgetting Katrine, asked questions about their new home, and speculated in excitement about the probabilities of there being salmon fishing in the neighbourhood.

His elders let him talk on. Jim was rather quiet and his sister wondered if he was thinking over Katrine's story. If he was, he made no further reference to her.

The train was only ten minutes late, but they were stiff and tired as they got out at the windy station.

Mary glanced at the sparse crowd leaving by the barrier. No sign of the rat-face man. He had mentioned Perth, but perhaps, after all, he was not getting out there.

The sun was going down slowly in pomp and splendour, and there was a fresh wind. Jim, handing out the tickets, was evidently planning the rest of the journey.

They were standing in a little group, their luggage round them, staring at the grey houses, hearing the soft Scottish voices on all sides, when a short, thick-set man in leggings and a pullover, carefully darned in numerous places, came stumping up to them.

"Will ye be the young folk for Lendaloch?" he asked, glancing from Jim to Mary and back again. Andrew was already getting entangled with his outsize fishing-rod which threatened to disintegrate from its bundle on his suitcase.

Jim brightened considerably. "Why yes, we are."

"The name's Ferguson, Jamie. Yon's the car waiting."

The car was a very ancient shooting-brake. It looked roomy enough to seat four people until Mary noticed, with some dismay, two heifer calves netted down at the end.

Jamie Ferguson swung wide the door by the driver.

"The lass can bide wi' me," he announced. "You twa lads willnae mind the wee cows."

"Is it far?" asked Andrew, hauling in his suitcase.

"Matter of twenty miles and a bit. Get ye in, all of ye."

Jim grinned. The luggage went in behind with the boys and Mary got in next to the driver. The heifers made a few complaining noises as they started with a jerk, but soon quietened as the car gathered speed.

Although she was enormously relieved that they were

to make the last lap of the journey without any tiresome changes on a train, Mary felt anxious. She had scarcely had time to look round the place to see if Katrine had been there. But then probably she had had to wait for another train, and even Jim felt that she was quite capable of making the journey under her own steam.

Meanwhile they were in the country again, taking a winding road past small stone-built farms, across rough moorland, once over a humped bridge, and on and on. Sometimes the sun was in their eyes, sometimes it cast deep shadows over the road when they thrust through a forest of thick pines.

They passed villages with white washed houses, old as time; they glimpsed distant water, but, always in the distance, were the rising hummocks of the moors, purple-tipped, some, the higher ones, wreathed in mist.

Behind, the boys began to sing, and sometimes the heifers mooed. The boys were singing Scottish songs— "Over the Sea to Skye" and "Will ye no come back again." The driver turned a seamed face to them, his wide mouth grinning.

"No sae bad for Sassenachs," he commented.

Mary had been so busy with her own thoughts that she had scarcely spoken to him.

"Do you live at Lendaloch?" she asked.

"Aye, in the village. Got a wee bit o' land, but I obleege the folks when so desired."

"I'm so glad you could meet us."

"'Tis a pleasure. The Auld Manse'll do weel to have young people aboot it. Yer mother's unco kind. Like a bairn she is, takin' in the beauty with real appreciation."

"It's going to be wonderful after London."

"Aye it will be that. I've nae use for the big toons."

"Do you know the castle?" asked Mary suddenly.

He did not answer as he manipulated the clumsy

vehicle past a boy driving a cow across the narrow road.

"Ye said?" he asked.

Mary repeated her question.

"The castle," he gave her a quick glance, "a fine place, empty now; forbye a fey place! Ye dinna want to gang there on yer ain."

"What's the matter with it?"

His eyes were on the road. "Naething, naething at all. There's some that says mair than their prayers, that's all, and the loch is deep, very deep, where the castle stands."

She had an impression, perhaps mistaken, that he didn't want to talk about the castle. But he seemed a practical man, not the type given to fancies. She said no more.

They were passing now through another village, deep in the moors, its stone houses on a winding main street; there were little shops and a large inn called, Mary noticed, The Lendaloch Arms. This must be Lendaloch, so they were nearly home.

She sat back, tense. Jamie Ferguson raised his hand to people who passed and who stared in at them with friendly curiosity.

Passing a boy who almost got under their wheels, a boy with wild fair hair, he shouted something, then turned to her.

"One of my ain lads."

"Have you a big family?"

"Five sons, 'twas the eldest there, courting disaster as usual on the road."

Up a hill between more firs, then down again and, suddenly to their left, water showed deep and dark, flecked, where the sunlight caught it, with vivid blue.

The loch itself?

To Mary's eyes it looked immense: a great sheet of

water stretching for miles. In reality it was, at that part, about a hundred and fifty yards across, though it widened farther on.

It looked very lonely, that sheet of water with, on the opposite side, a fringe of trees and, beyond that, what looked like a mountain, its head in clouds.

"What is that?" she asked.

"Benavar. 'Tis to be fine forbye. Mist brings fine weather and her head's wreathed in mist."

Oddly enough they reached the end of their journey almost before they realised.

Their driver abruptly turned the car up a narrow lane, then out on to a broader thoroughfare which brought them back again to what seemed the very verge of the loch.

Then they saw it: the drive gates painted a pleasant green, and a garden with a neat lawn sweeping down to the road. The house stood well back: it was of grey stone, its three peaked roofs rising steeply above deep-set windows; creeper covered the walls, but the windows shone in the light of the sun and, in front of the door, was a large pantechnicon.

"That's guid," remarked Jamie Ferguson as he drew up, "yer mother was anxious about the furniture and all." He gave Mary a quick smile, "She'll be glad to have you around to gie her a hand."

They tumbled out, the boys stopping to stare, then Andrew ran ahead to the door, for there was Mother, wearing an overall and a scarf round her hair, racing to meet them, followed more sedately by her friend whom they had learned to call Aunt Lilian.

Mrs. Carew kissed Mary, and hugged the boys.

"Here you are at last! I can't believe it. Darlings, you'll be tired and hungry so we'll call it a day soon. The furniture, our own, that is, has just come."

They all entered the wide square hall, which was oak-pannelled, with doors to unexplored rooms on either side. A shallow staircase led to the upper floors, but, for the time being, they only stared around them whilst two laconic men moved in furniture, returning to their mother for instructions.

Mrs. Carew laughed. "You see what it's like! You go with Aunt Lilian to the kitchen and she'll find you some food. I'll have to stand by for a bit."

Jim elected to stand by, too, but Mary was persuaded to follow Mrs. Hames with Andrew to the large kitchen. She stared around her, taking in the huge dresser, where china and glass stood as yet unarranged, and the big stove which glowed redly. Next to it was an electric stove, though it did not seem to be in use, and there was an outsize table scrubbed white, and half a dozen chairs.

"You'll be starving." Lilian Hames, a slight, grey-haired woman with clear-cut features and a sweet smile, was already flinging a cloth on the table.

"You needn't worry, Aunt Lilian," said Mary, "we had a huge meal on the train; in fact there's a hamper somewhere with lots left in it . . ." she broke off.

"What's the matter, dear?"

"My friend Katrine. She broke her journey. I suppose she hasn't rung up?"

"Katrine, of course! Your mother told me. She's coming on later? Can she find her way alone?"

"I expect so." It was no use going into explanations, but as she drank tea and ate the cold meat and salad put before them, she was still worrying about Katrine.

They explored their new home and Mother told them all about it; how Lilian had had this legacy and how she had insisted that the Carew family come and live here with her to see if they could make it a going concern.

But as she listened, always at the back of Mary's mind was the little nagging worry about Katrine and her whereabouts.

But when the men departed with their pantechnicon, there was so much to see, so much to do that there were moments when the sheer wonder of it all took first place.

Mrs. Hames had been lucky, she declared. She had bought a good deal of the furniture which went with the place, and consequently the eight rooms were adequately furnished; although she might have to buy more beds and bedding if they got more guests than expected.

"Technically there are eight rooms," she said, as they went to the first floor, "two really large ones here in front, two smaller at the back, and four above, though they are smaller too; and we have three garret rooms which we can use if we are full up." She laughed. "I'm so happy for you all. Come and see your own rooms."

Mary had a little room to herself on the second floor, adjoining her mother's and Lilian's, and the boys shared a larger one. The furniture was old-fashioned—there were washhand-stands with ewers and bowls, instead of the fitted running water bowls in most hotels. That, Lilian, decided, would have to come later.

"At the beginning it will be hard work replenishing water and taking up hot water to the guests," she said, "but we have two bathrooms after all."

Mary walked up and down stairs, and peeped in and out of rooms happily: she liked the panelled walls below, the pale cream paint and gay papers in all the rooms, she even liked the large wardrobes and old dressing-tables with their many drawers, the rather worn carpets on landings, the many coloured rugs, also worn, on the polished floors. To her, after living in a four-roomed flat in London it seemed a huge place, from the three, small, sloped-roofed rooms of the garrets, the windows of which gave a wonderful view across the loch, to the spacious ground-floor rooms.

Already the place spoke of home, for Mother had had her piano brought into the lounge, and packing cases waited there containing her treasured china and other odds and ends such as the photographs of the family and the few good etchings which had belonged to their father. The two main rooms faced the main road across the garden, but Mother had taken one room at the back, a smaller one over the kitchen garden and orchard, for their own use.

"In the winter we have the run of the house, but, in the summer, we shall want a place of our own," she said, then turning to Mary, "Darling, are you going to like it?"

"It's heavenly, Mum. But isn't it going to be a lot of work? Oh, I mean we'll help all we can when we're here, but all those stairs and rooms!"

Mother tapped her cheek. "What a worry you are. Lilian and I can manage between us, and Jamie has found us a very nice woman, a relative of his I dare say, who will come in daily when we're settled, to help with the rough."

"I'm so glad."

They were in the big lounge which was furnished with deep, comfortable armchairs, a wide settee, little tables, and a window-seat round the big windows.

Jim, who had been helping unpack, came in and stood by the window staring out.

"I say," he remarked, "that must be the castle. Look, Mary."

Mary moved to his side. The sun was fading and the loch looked cold like slate under the slight wind. Almost opposite showed a grey building, a tower against the night sky, square and somehow important, although it was well over a hundred yards across the water.

"Katrine's Castle," murmured Mary.

Her mother came up to them. "Yes, when is Katrine coming?" she asked, "did you say that she has something to do with the castle?"

"She lived there," said Mary, all her anxiety returning.

Mrs. Carew frowned. "Surely it was not her father who disappeared so mysteriously? Lilian heard something about it in the village."

"Yes." Mary nodded.

"Oh, I gather that it's a big place but unoccupied now, and the old part has an odd name with people round here. Especially since this happened."

If Mother noticed something in both their faces which puzzled her, she said nothing.

"Poor child, I'm not sure it's good for her to be here after what has happened. All the same we'll do our best to make her happy," she went on.

Before night really fell Andrew, who had been exploring the garden, begged them to come out with him. There was an orchard and lots of windfalls already, he said, and there were raspberries too.

The kitchen garden had been well kept up: there were potatoes as yet undug, cabbages uncut, even a trench ready for celery, whilst the flower garden was a mass of summer flowers, phlox, hibiscus and roses, many roses, as this part of the world was well-sheltered and was what Jamie called a suntrap.

Really they were all very tired, even though they had done nothing but sit in a train all day, and their mother tried to persuade them to get to bed.

Mary ached with weariness, her head whirled with all she had seen, and all she had yet to see of their new home, but, as she went into the big hall, now untidy with rolls of carpet, packing cases and the like, she glanced at the silent telephone on its table by the door.

Katrine would be able to ring them surely, for she knew the Manse and would have no difficulty in getting the number. She had not done so.

What had happened to her?

CHAPTER FOUR

A DAY OF SURPRISES

MARY SLEPT deeply, as they all did. But she awoke early in the unfamiliar room, feeling first surprise, because they were here at the Manse, then delight, because the sun shone with a brightness she had never known in London. Then came a feeling that there was something to worry about, and she remembered.

Katrine had not arrived, neither had she rung up. Mary glanced at her watch: it was only a few minutes after six. She got up and padded over to the window. Her room looked across the back garden to the rise covered with spruce firs, fresh and green and feathery; every leaf, every blade of grass glistened, and beyond, far beyond, rose the towering peak of Benavar, to-day undimmed by mist. A myriad of birds cheeped, and, as she watched, a grey squirrel raced across the potato patch and ran up the bark of an old apple tree.

It was a morning to be outside. Mary pulled out her, as yet, unpacked case and found some old slacks and a tee-shirt, then hurried along to the bathroom on her floor to wash.

No one seemed to be up and she felt a little triumphant when, dressed, she found her way down to the kitchen, peeping as she went into the spacious living-rooms. The rooms were theirs, even if they did have to share them with guests sooner or later. It was going to be wonderful. If only Katrine were all right.

She stared at the stove which was always kept on to feed the rather primitive hot-water system, found their electric kettle, and switched it on.

She was finding cups and saucers, and had discovered a half-pound packet of tea in some triumph, when the kitchen door opened and she started.

"Beat you to it. Gosh but it's cold."

Jim stood there, old dressing-gown over his bathing trunks.

"Good heavens, you haven't been in the loch?"

"I have, and believe you me, it's icy." He held out a goose-pimpled arm. "But it was worth it—most invigorating."

"And I thought I was the first one up!"

"Never mind, you're being domesticated, your mind on tea. Me first, please."

She made the tea in the big aluminium teapot which had come with the rest of their own things, then began to lay a tray. She handed a cup of tea to her brother.

"I'm worried about Katrine."

Jim gulped down the tea. "Same here. Still I should think she'll be all right."

"She should have been here by ten, or telephoned."

"I know, still don't meet troubles half-way. Me for a bath and a shave."

"Shave!"

He felt his chin on which the slightest rash of hairs was evident. "Oh, I shave, didn't you know?"

Mary giggled, was glared at for her pains, then quickly finished laying the tray and took it up to her mother's room.

Mrs. Carew was already up, and stood fully dressed by the window whilst Lilian, in her dressing-gown, was sitting by the bed.

"We should get some answers any time now," she was saying. They were discussing their project, of course.

Mary put down the tray.

"I thought I was up first, but Jim beat me to it. Actually he's been for a bathe in the loch."

Mother smiled. "Good. Oh, it's going to be wonderful for you kids."

Lilian took a cup. "Anything wrong, chick?" she asked Mary.

"Yes, I'm wondering about Katrine. She should have been here last night."

"Katrine? But she's coming to-day. Darling, she rang from a hotel, in Perth, I think. It was almost eleven but Lilian and I stayed up to do some unpacking long after you three were in bed."

Mary glowed. "Then she's all right?"

"Of course. She sent her love to you and said that everything was all right, whatever that meant. She'll be here by midday, perhaps earlier. I've rung Ferguson to take the car in for her."

Lilian had been watching her in some curiosity. "You seem very anxious about your friend, dear."

"I am—I was, I mean. But she's all right now."

She left them and went back to finish her unpacking, humming to herself as she put her clothes into the huge wardrobe, and her toilet articles on the old walnut dressing-table.

She had almost finished when the two boys burst in. Andrew was full of news.

"I've been exploring the grounds," he said grandly. "There's a little stream at the end of the garden, and I saw a stag beyond the woods."

"You *think* you saw one."

"And *I'm* getting up early to-morrow for a swim," Andrew said, drawing himself up. "I'm hungry. By the way, when's breakfast?"

They took their breakfast at eight o'clock in the kitchen as none of the other rooms was ready. There were new-laid eggs from Ferguson's farm, thick slices of home-cured bacon, and, to follow, raspberry jam sent by Mrs. Ferguson from her own store.

"People are nice," commented Mary, "I thought the Scots considered the English poor Sassenachs."

Lilian smiled. "You mustn't think any such thing. We're a warm-hearted race. Still," she went on seriously, "there are many poor people in the village. Far poorer than those down south. I think they miss the Maclure, as they call him, very much. He was very good to them."

"Katrine's father! Aunt Lilian, have you heard what really happened to him?"

"Only what Jamie Ferguson told us. He left the castle one evening only a few weeks ago, in mid-June it would be. He had been entertaining some guest, but next morning there was no sign of him anywhere and his bed had not been slept in. He has never been seen since, and he was expecting guests later that month, too. He just vanished."

"Never been heard of since!" quoted Andrew thoughtlessly.

Mary quelled him with a look. "And no trace of him was found?"

"Oh the police were called in, they are still looking for him. The loch was dragged, at least by the shores, for it is very deep. But he was a good swimmer from all accounts." She shook her head, "No one can understand it at all."

Mother looked unhappy. "That poor child. What does she hope to do by coming here?"

Mary shook her head, and Jim looked sober, then said, "I suppose she'll make inquiries to try and find out more. But I'm sorry for her, and of course I'll help her all I can."

Mary looked at him in some surprise. Jim as a kind of knight errant was strange to her.

Her mother said quickly, "What we must do is make her as happy as we can, try and take her mind off it, though that is going to be difficult. Frankly I don't think it's a good idea."

"What, Mummy?"

"That she should come here where, of course, she must have been so happy with her father. Thank goodness we're a family. We can cheer her up and try to stop her from brooding."

They were all rather quiet, and, as Mary helped clear and wash up, she realised more than ever what her friend would have to face.

The morning passed quickly. The place had to be thoroughly cleaned before the new furniture was put into position. Carpets were taken up and put out on the lawn, and while Mary helped her mother and Lilian wash and scour and polish the floors, the boys beat the carpets, and took out all the packing cases to store in the big shed outside the kitchen where the fuel and wood was kept. China and glass, and pots and pans were all put on the table in the kitchen to be cleaned, but they all downed tools for a cup of tea and biscuits when the post came.

The postman was elderly and taciturn; instead of coming round to the front he sauntered into the yard and walked into the kitchen.

"Mrs. Hames, Mrs. Carew," he announced, slamming some letters on the cluttered table. "Weel, weel, what a pother, at sixes and sevens, eh?"

"We'll soon be to rights," said Mother.

"Aye"—he paused—"anythin' ye'll be wishin' from doon yonder?"

Mary was puzzled for she had yet to learn that the

postman took orders and obliged with messages by word of mouth in that part of the world.

"I don't think so."

"McGregor's got some fine steak. Too expensive I told him for us folk. Maybe ye'd be likin' some?"

"All right, tell him we'll have a pound."

"Seven shillings the pound, it is."

"Well, stewing steak then."

He nodded and left them reluctantly. Mother glanced through the mail. Some letters were personal, but two were from prospective guests.

"A Colonel and Mrs. Brayne would like to know if they can have a private sitting-room—can we manage that, Lilian?"

Lilian considered. "They could have the back room off the stairs, better say yes. Two pounds a week extra."

Mary had been dipping as well. "Here's an old lady, a Mrs. Hamilton who wants to bring her companion, and she has a dog, too."

Mother took the letter. "Now off you run, all of you. Mary, have you seen to Katrine's room? Good. We'll have to get down to these." She stopped and took up a third letter. The postmark was that of Dunraven on the other side of the loch.

"Funny, I wonder who this is. A man who signs himself Giles Canning. One room, that should be easy."

None of them were listening. In fact as they moved to the front of the house to bring some kind of order to the main sitting-room, Andrew said:

"I think it's ghastly having a lot of strangers in."

"We have to," Mary told him, "if we want to keep this as our home we've got to take people in the season."

"When's that?"

"Well, I suppose from April to October."

"Oh, heck." Then he brightened. "That leaves out Christmas, anyway."

At the time of speaking, Christmas, naturally enough, seemed a very long time off.

Mary was watching the time—it was nearly eleven and Katrine should arrive soon now. She found herself staring out at the drive, watching for the shabby shooting brake which had brought them here last night.

But as luck would have it she was at the back of the house, looking for a treasured picture which seemed to have gone astray when Andrew came racing in.

"She's come!"

Mary hurried round the house to the front and there was Ferguson negotiating his clumsy vehicle up the drive, and there was Katrine, looking pale but quite collected, waving from it.

The man had plenty to say, as usual, and, as Mary ran up, he rummaged in the back of the car and brought out a small wicker-basket.

"Boodle," he announced. "I told yer mother all about her. Got a bit of Siamese in her, but a wonderful one for the mice and her only three months. Smallest of the litter, she was, but a nice wee thing."

Mary stared and Katrine looked on with amusement as plaintive mews came from the basket.

"A cat!" exclaimed Mary.

"I told ye, yer guid mother's goin' to gie it a hame." He grinned, got into the driving-seat, took Katrine's generous tip without effusion, and drove away.

And so it was that Katrine arrived with Boodle the kitten and the introductions were somewhat confused.

"This is Katrine, Mummy," Mary said, as they came into the hall, "and Ferguson's brought a cat."

She had forgotten that Andrew adored cats above all animals. As Katrine was greeting Mrs. Carew and

Lilian, he had the basket open and out sprang a kitten, a dark-brown tortoise-shell with a tiny yellow mark on her nose.

Andrew just gathered her up and disappeared; and for the rest of the day his work suffered, as he seemed to be constantly losing the little creature and finding it again.

Meanwhile Katrine was shown up to her room. Mary left her with her mother and came down to get more tea and find out what they could do about lunch: after all Katrine was their first guest.

When they came down she saw that Katrine and her mother had taken to each other. They were smiling and Katrine was talking brightly as though no shadow lay over her visit here.

Not until after lunch when, by common consent, they relaxed a little before a further onslaught on the work still to be done, did Mary have a chance of talking to Katrine alone. They strolled round the garden and across the road to the verge of the loch, lapping now in the sunlight, its opposite side hazy in the heat of the afternoon.

"We had such a fright," Mary told her. "That man wasn't in his place and we were sure he'd followed you after all. Then he came up and actually asked us the time."

"I was very careful," Katrine told her, "but I had to wait for quite a time for the next train to Perth, then it seemed to take absolutely hours. When I got there I went straight to a hotel, had a meal and went to bed. I was in two minds," she added, "whether to ring up, for it was jolly late when I did."

"I'm glad you did," Mary told her, "I was very worried about you and so was Jim."

Katrine laughed. "Oh, Jim! He's like you, isn't he,

Mary? I mean in character, of course. Kind of wholesome and dependable."

"Thank you for those few kind words," said Mary, inwardly wondering what her brother would say if he'd heard those two words applied to him.

They stood by the loch and Katrine stared across the water. In the distance a couple of boats moved slowly to the other bank, and as they watched, a small schooner raced along in the distance, its wake slowly reaching their shore and disturbing the rushes there.

"Your castle is quite clear to-day," said Mary.

"Yes, but that's the old part, the tower. I should think it's five hundred years old, though well preserved. The new part was added in the time of Charles II. I think the Maclure of that time had helped him, and the money he received went towards the new building."

"I say, how interesting!"

"Yes." There was a sadness on Katrine's face as she looked across towards that distant tower, and Mary was reminded with some misgiving of the reason for her stay here.

"To-morrow, perhaps, we'll go and look at it," said Katrine. "The caretaker and his wife are living there, or rather they live at the lodge. I want to go through it."

"Why?"

Katrine turned and her eyes were dark, her mouth set. "I want to explore the old tower thoroughly. The Room of the Mirror is there, so they say."

"What is it like?"

The other shook her head. "I don't know. Father wouldn't let me go all over it because parts of it are unsafe."

"Promise me something," Mary implored.

"What?"

"You'll never, on any account, go there by yourself."

Katrine shook her head. "Easy. I wouldn't dare. Perhaps to-morrow you and Jim could come with me."

"Of course we will." Mary spoke soberly. It would all have been very exciting had she not known what lay behind Katrine's quest.

They went back to the house and Katrine insisted on helping. By evening the big sitting-room was ready for the most critical of visitors, glowing with polish, the radio installed, even favourite books on the many shelves on either side of the hearth.

Upstairs the bedrooms were taking shape and when they at last sat down to their meal in the dining-room, (a somewhat austere place with heavy sideboard, huge table and a positive regiment of straight-backed chairs), their elders discussed the applications for rooms they had received.

Mrs. Carew and Lilian had decided to accept the colonel and his wife, also the old lady and her companion.

"I hope they'll fit in," said Lilian, "but we must start as soon as we can. Anyhow they sound nice, quiet people."

Andrew, who was surreptitiously feeding Boodle, the little cat which had already adopted him, gave an audible sigh.

"There's this man, Canning," went on Lilian. "He said he'd ring to-night for particulars. Perhaps I shall be able to tell from his voice the type he is."

Katrine laughed. "Why worry, Mrs. Hames. He's probably some tourist who's heard of this place by chance."

"I know. I shouldn't be so fussy. But in a guest-house like this one has to try and get people who fit in together."

The young people were quickly bored with the discussion—to the boys the guests were a necessary evil, and to Mary, just people. She liked people, they interested her; and it would be fun, a word she frequently used, to receive them and make them happy.

They were all tired at the end of a very active day, and went to bed about ten, even although the light had not yet faded. Katrine, whose room was next to Mary's, came in to say good night.

"I'm so glad I've come," she said, "I like you all so much. Your mother's a dear."

"That's good."

"Sometimes I wish it were somewhere else. I keep remembering." She stood looking out of the wide-open window at the orchard and woods below. Soon it would be dusk, and already the sound of owls, of which there were many, broke the silence.

"That motor-launch we saw this afternoon, Father was going to get one this summer."

"I'm so sorry, Katrine. Try not to grieve," said Mary, feeling inadequate.

"I know. Still, to-morrow—have you told Jim about going to the castle to-morrow?"

"Yes, he insists on coming. In fact he seems to think you shouldn't go near there alone."

"Nice of him. Well, I shan't."

Katrine went out and Mary heard her opening her own window next door before she lay down and prepared to sleep.

She did not seem to have been asleep for more than a few minutes when she was wakened rather frighteningly by someone standing by her bed. She sat up quickly.

"Who's that?"

"It's me, Andrew. Mary, have you a torch?"

"What on earth for?"

"It's Boodle, I left her in her box in the kitchen as

Mum told me, then I got to thinking she might want some more milk so I went down."

Went down no doubt to bring her up to his room. Mary smiled in the darkness—she knew Andrew.

"Mary, the window was open, she must have got out. I've got to find her—she's so small, the owls may get her."

Mary got up and found her dressing-gown and slippers. Apart from the fact that she hated to think of the little thing wandering off and getting lost, she knew only too well that Andrew would not rest until his kitten was found.

"The owls won't get her, silly, but we'd better have a look. There's a torch in the sideboard drawer, I put it there to-day. Now, don't waken people up."

Together they crept down the stairs in the darkness. Mary felt her way across the dining-room, colliding on the way with one of the many chairs, and finally found the torch. They let themselves out by the kitchen door and into the soft darkness.

It was quite warm, and the smell of the loch and of green things, was pleasant. Calling, "Boodle" not too loudly, they circled the kitchen garden, Andrew going one way, Mary the other.

Mary moved through the orchard, casting her torch beam before her and was on the verge of the woods when she heard a rustle quite near.

"Boodle," she called, then: "Is that you, Andy?"

Abruptly a shadow split itself from the shadows of the spruce firs and a man stood there towering over her. Mary recoiled, her throat dry, and stifled a scream.

"It's all right. Sorry I startled you."

The voice was friendly, the accent Scottish, and her wavering torchlight showed her a tall, thin tweed-clad man with what looked like a sandy moustache.

She retreated in spite of his apparent friendliness. He paced after her until they reached the garden.

"You the new people here?" he asked.

"Yes, we only came yesterday."

"I did hear it was going to be a guest-house. Got any yet?"

"No, not yet."

"But Miss Maclure is with you?"

"She's a school friend of mine, as it happens."

"I see." Mary wished Andrew would come but he seemed to have quite disappeared. All the same the stranger seemed harmless enough, though inquisitive.

He stood, a large shadow, eyes shrewd in his thin face. "Looking for someone?"

"A kitten."

There was a smile in his voice as he said, "Well, don't let me keep you from your search."

He turned and left her, walking towards the woods.

Mary went back to the garden and almost ran into Andrew as he came rushing forward.

"Found her," he announced, "she was circling round on the lawn. Wanted a game, I ask you!"

He hurried into the house ahead of her, taking his pet up to his own room, Mary suspected.

She crept up the stairs and had reached her room door when she saw that the light was on there and she had not switched it on.

Katrine stood by the window, and turned quickly as Mary came in. "Mary, you've been out! You were talking to someone."

"Yes, Andrew lost his kitten and we were looking for her."

"Who were you talking to?"

"I don't know, a man. He came out of the wood. He was quite all right, though curious about us."

"What was he like or was it too dark to see?"

"Tall, thin, tweedy, a moustache and I think he was fair. What's the matter, Katrine?"

"I only wondered if perhaps it was the man who followed me."

"Of course not. He was Scottish for one thing and I'd have known the man on the train at once."

Katrine made a noise like a laugh.

"Guess I've got too much imagination. Now get to bed; do you know it's nearly midnight?"

Poor Katrine! As she lay down again Mary reflected that they must, as Jim had said, keep with her as much as they could. Either there was some danger threatening her or the uncertainty about her father's fate was getting the better of her.

All the same the stranger she had encountered in the dark had been a very different kind of person from the one on the train; he had, in fact, been rather pleasant.

CHAPTER FIVE

THEY COME TO THE CASTLE

THE NEXT day Katrine seemed almost cheerful, talking with Jim about their experiences in taking their G.C.E.

"I took chemistry and physics and Latin," she declared over breakfast.

"What would a girl like you want with Latin?" Jim teased her.

"Well, it's the root of so many words," she said firmly, "After all, the Romans lived in Britain and the language is steeped in the Latin they spoke. And French and German."

"Have it your own way. Anyway I took Latin, too."

"Well you're going to be a doctor, aren't you?"

Jim sobered. "That depends."

Listening Mary remembered that her brother had talked of shelving his ambition in order to start work at eighteen, and she decided to talk it over with her mother.

Katrine insisted on helping that morning, for there was still much to do: a house with eight bedrooms, not to mention four sitting-rooms, takes some settling into.

In the end Mary allowed Katrine to unpack and arrange the last box of books, whilst she went into the kitchen to see if there was anything for Jim to get from the shops. His and Andrew's bicycles had come with the furniture, and they were both eager to go into the village.

A list was made and off they went, and Mary went to the upper rooms with her mother to help her arrange furniture, store the unpacked linen in a big cupboard in the first floor bathroom, and generally make herself useful.

"Lilian has answered both those applications," Mother remarked, as she shook her head over a pair of torn sheets and put them aside for mending. "But that man who wrote, the Canning man, hasn't rung up. Probably he's found something else. I expect we'll have more inquiries though."

"I know it's going to be a success."

"No reason why it shouldn't be. You've no idea what it's like for me to leave London and that office for ever, darling."

"I know, Mum, I'm so glad for you."

"I like your Katrine very much, by the way. She's thoughtful and, I'd say, very clever."

"Oh, she is."

"She seems to be settling down very nicely."

"I know. We're going to the castle this afternoon."

Mrs. Carew looked doubtful, "Must you?"

"She's determined about it. We'll all go, Jim, Andrew and myself."

Mother said nothing more for, glancing out of the narrow window which overlooked the drive, they saw the postman cycling round.

He was entering the kitchen when they got there, and he touched his cap and put down some letters as well as a much wrapped parcel of meat.

"Meat," he announced. "'Tis what you ordered yesterday; pound of best stewing, four shillings and threepence, and he put in a couple of kidneys which are one and fourpence, making in all five shillings and sevenpence. An awful lot of money, I'd say."

As her mother went to get her purse Mary turned over the letters and asked:

"Do you know a tall man with a moustache, who lives round here?"

The postman's bright eyes considered her.

"Could be Murdo—he has a boat or two down by the loch—he has a moustache. . . ."

"I don't think so somehow, he didn't speak like a Scot —well, not really."

The man she had encountered last night had been no fisherman, as his accent had shown. The postman was sharp enough to guess what she meant.

"You mean 'twas one of the gentry? Since the Maclure went—and he wasna moustached—I don't know one like that. Would he be auld or young?"

She was at a disadvantage. "Not old exactly . . . he might have been anything from thirty-five to forty."

"Ye arna observant, are ye?"

Mary gave up. She could not go into long explanations about her encounter with the stranger in the dark. It was obvious the little postman knew everyone in the district and her vague description had definitely not rung a bell.

As he received his money and turned to go he said, "I'll make inquiries, but 'tis likely 'twas a stranger passin' through."

Mary turned, for someone else had come into the kitchen and stood by the dresser. It was Katrine and she had evidently been listening to the exchange.

"Funny Sandy didn't know the man, Mary. Are you sure he wasn't one of the people round here?"

"Well, he had a cultured voice, with a touch of Scots in it. I would say he was a gentleman."

"Oh, I expect he was passing through as Sandy said. Come and see the books, I'm not sure I've arranged them to your liking."

So Mary came and approved Katrine's arrangement of

the book-shelves; Mother's favourite books on one side, hers and the boys' on the other, with the school and text-books Jim seemed to have collected, below.

The boys returned to find them busy. Jim had made acquaintance, it seemed, with half the village; the baker was calling and MacDonald's farm would supply their milk and butter.

"I didn't mention eggs as Ferguson does those. I like the people, they aren't exactly chatty but they're most terribly polite." He grinned at Katrine. "The owner of the general shop and post office is a Latin student, very well educated."

"I know. That will be Angus Lowther, he went to Glasgow University. He was to be a doctor but his two brothers were killed in the war and he had to manage the store for his mother."

"What a shame."

"Perhaps. I think he's a happy man really. His little wife's a darling and he's got two lovely children."

Watching Katrine, Mary realised that she was really interested in people, people for whom her father had felt himself responsible as the principal landowner there.

Over lunch, which Lilian had prepared—a simple lunch of salad from the garden and cold ham, followed by raspberries and the top of the milk—they discussed their expedition that afternoon.

"The castle looks miles away," said Andrew, "how do we get there?"

"It's quickest by boat, but that would mean getting Fergus, who has the boat-house down by the loch, to row us over. I suggest we walk this time."

"Is it a long walk?"

"About three miles perhaps, as we have to skirt the loch of course. We'll approach it from the south. It'll be a scramble." Katrine smiled at Mary, "Slacks I'd say, and tough shoes."

It was well after two when they all started off, for, at the last minute, Andrew missed his beloved Boodle, and she had to be found and entrusted to his mother's care before he was ready to come with them.

Katrine led the way down the road by the loch then up a rise beyond, taking what seemed little better than a sheep track which ran between the hummocks of the lower moorland. For a time all sight of the water was lost to them and they seemed to be walking in a maze of hills, the sun casting a short shadow in front of them.

Katrine was very quiet, a slim figure in slacks and pullover, her dark hair in one long plait bobbing on her shoulders. For a time there seemed no end to the pleasant wilderness about them, with now and then a vagrant little burn which followed them in the dips.

Every now and then Andrew would ask: "Are we far from the castle?"

"This is a short-cut," Katrine told him briefly, and Jim had something critical to say about all short-cuts.

They had been walking for half an hour or perhaps more when Katrine paused a moment.

"When we top that rise beyond we'll be in sight of the other side of the loch."

Imperceptibly the country was changing; coloured crags topped the hillside, and heather lay in patches only on barren slopes. It was warm, and the damp heat gave birth, it seemed, to a myriad of winged creatures: bees among the heather, butterflies and tiny day moths, troublesome horseflies. Once they saw a kestrel circling high above them, ignoring a lark which spun its little song beyond the clouds. This was Scotland, untouched as it had been for centuries. Mary looked around her with a kind of awe. It was a wild country and untamed, very different from the placid fields and low hills of England.

"By the way," said Andrew as they clambered on, "I saw some police in a launch this morning, three of them. They were circling the loch."

"Shut up," muttered Jim, glancing at Katrine's slim figure ahead of them.

"Why?"

"Probably still searching for her father, ass! He hasn't been traced and it's coming on to a month now."

Mary went a little cold. The search would go on, but what would they find? She was glad Katrine had not heard the exchange.

They were climbing another rise, and, reaching the top, they found themselves looking down on a fairer landscape. A valley lay below, a fertile valley, thick with trees; beyond showed water, blue now as the sky it reflected: the loch again, and, this time, from the opposite shore.

"Look, I can see our house!" cried Andrew. He was right. Across the calm waters their new home showed, its three steep gables backed by the mountain of Benavar deceptively near.

"Let's get on," said Katrine and began the descent. They were soon moving between firs which fringed the shores of the loch, dark firs, their needles making a soft mesh carpet. Presently they reached a path which wound downwards. Katrine moved quickly round trees and between crags and still they could see no sign of the castle.

Jim was saying something sarcastic about short-cuts again, when Katrine led the way through a grove of larches to a small peninsula which projected over the loch, and, dramatically they had their first glimpse of the tall, grey tower of the castle.

They stopped a moment and stared up at the narrow

windows of that ancient keep, for Lendaloch, immediately above the loch itself and rising from the rocks as if part of them, looked both beautiful and grim.

Katrine spoke quietly. "That's the old part of course. The main part, which we lived in, is on the other side."

Mary still stared at the grey mass, the slit-like windows looking, she thought imaginatively, like half-shut eyes.

"Let's get on for goodness' sake," said Jim.

Following Katrine they skirted the edge, then another scramble along the rough edge of the loch brought them down to a road which led west and away from the loch itself in a semi-circle. Mary was inclined to stare across, far across, to the distant peaked roofs which were now home. The nearer she got to Katrine's castle the less she liked the look of it.

They were now following a low stone wall which must be round the park of the castle; it was broken at last by lodge gates with, to one side, a small grey house which was the lodge itself.

Katrine opened a tiny gate painted white and went up the path to knock. They stood waiting, staring at the closed windows, neatly curtained; and were stared at in turn by an errant chicken which seemed to have escaped from its run.

Katrine knocked again, waited, then came back.

"That's funny, the Nicholsons should be at home. Unless they've gone away to their son in England. Father used to let them holiday there now and then, I know."

"What are you going to do then?" asked Jim.

"Go up to the castle of course. Come on, everybody."

Nobody spoke as they made their way up the great drive which wound between rough parkland, high with bracken and thickly wooded. Andrew exclaimed when a couple of fallow deer stared at them from a glade, but Katrine walked on until an abrupt turn brought them within sight of the gracious façade of the house. The tower showed far to the left, and the house itself was, as Katrine had said, of a much later period. It was a lovely example of Stuart architecture, high-paned windows under a beautifully etched roof, with a curved stairway up to a terrace. The main door was itself under a magnificent oriel window. The beauty of the long double line of those windows was enhanced by the lawn in front, wide and green, sweeping down to the parkland.

From this part of the house there was no sign of the loch which lay to their left where the tower brooded.

Katrine climbed the arched stairway to the great door, glanced back at them, shrugged, then pulled the bell at the side.

Reaching her side they could hear it pealing in the great house.

They waited for a minute, two, three. Katrine rang again impatiently, rapped on the big bronze knocker which was carved in the shape of a falcon's head, then she stood back to scan the windows. They were all blank though they shone in the sunlight; the place seemed absolutely deserted.

"What are you going to do?" asked Mary.

Katrine frowned at the shut door.

"I'll have to break in, I suppose." Turning she led the way along the terrace and round to the back of the great place.

They all stared with interest at the numerous outbuildings which were ranged round three sides of a paved courtyard behind the castle. There were old stables, with no horses, a newly-built garage with no cars, ancient stone-built store-houses, and, beyond these, on the left rose the rough walls of the tower with narrow windows, and high, rugged walls. Here the ground-floor windows, narrow and deeply set, were shuttered with rough planks of wood fitted to them and wedged in. The narrow wooden door, nail-studded, which gave on to the court-yard, was locked fast. Jim tried it and looked at Katrine.

"Tough proposition, this. How are we to get in? And, anyhow, do we want to?"

"I want to."

"Why not wait until the caretakers come back? The people in the village will probably know when they are returning."

But Katrine was pacing away to the back of the newer part of the building. Here was another door with a modern mortice lock. It, too, was locked but next to it showed a window.

She turned to Jim. "This window gives on to the pantry. Got a knife?"

Without speaking, although he looked as though he had no liking for the job, Jim took out his penknife and inserted it in the lintel, forced it, and the window swung inwards. He turned.

"Andrew, you climb up and through. Can do?"

Andrew was only too eager. "Sure!"

He was up and through it in a moment. In a creditably short time he had the door open and they all trooped in, finding themselves in a stone-flagged passage which led into a huge and lofty kitchen. Again Katrine took the lead, and crossing this, followed another passage which led from the kitchen to a green-covered baize door.

She swung it wide and they entered a large galleried hall from which the principal rooms of the newer part of the castle opened.

They stared around them. The great hall, with a black and red marble floor, was in perfect order. There were heavy rugs, two large tables ranged on either side of a deep hearth at one end, easy-chairs, even books and magazines were on the tables.

Oddly silent, Katrine began to open doors, and enter room after room, drawing aside the thick tapestry curtains which shrouded the tall, graceful windows, letting light in, then passing on to the next room.

Jim glanced at his sister; but she said nothing. Now that she was in the Castle of Lendaloch she felt depressed as well as impressed. It seemed so strange, even a little frightening, that all this should belong to Katrine.

The rooms were immense: there was a great library, the windows of which looked across the lawn to the park; and a drawing-room furnished with gilded French furniture with golden tapestry on the walls which opened from the gallery above, and took up a quarter of the first floor.

There were fourteen bedrooms, some formally furnished in fairly modern fashion, two large ones with four-poster beds in which Charles II himself might have slept and perhaps had, and, at the top of the house, ten other bedrooms probably once used by the servants.

The whole place gave Mary, at least, an impression of waiting, as though it indeed waited for a concourse of people from another day to come into its rooms, eat there and make merry, sleep in the great beds. But it had an untenanted look, sheets and blankets were stored away in great presses, mattresses turned up and over.

On the ground floor there were many small rooms off the hall, tiny ante-rooms, a gun room, billiard and smoking rooms, the latter full of fishing-tackle which made Andrew's eyes pop.

Katrine left the best for the last.

Turning along the gallery again, she opened double doors at the end.

"This is the old ballroom and picture gallery," she said.

She had been listening to their comments in silence.

They all stared at the expanse of polished floor. It was lit by eight great windows which gave upon the front of the house, and four chandeliers, their Venetian glass lustres shining, were suspended from a high, carved ceiling.

On the walls were portraits: a tall, proud-looking man, his hair tied back from his aquiline face wearing the kilt of the clan, was the Maclure who had followed the young Charles into exile, Katrine explained. Next to him a heavy-faced man in a full-bottomed wig stared down at them, and beside him, his lady—pale, small of mouth, wearing a blue, silken, low-necked dress. Her hair was powdered and a ringlet lay on her shoulder.

The boys moved along, studying the portraits.

Katrine took Mary's arm. "Come with me," she said.

She led the way out to another door following a passage which found them at right angles to the hall. A sudden turn brought them to another passage, narrow and dark: at the end was a curtained doorway.

It was very still. Mary glanced over her shoulder almost nervously and was relieved to see that the boys had followed them and were coming up.

Katrine was drawing the heavy curtain, behind which was an iron-studded door.

She turned the ancient handle, but it would not move. Jim came up and took it from her, pushed and pummelled, but still it would not move.

"It must be barred from the other side," he said. "Anyhow, where does it lead to?"

"To the tower," Katrine explained. "It is usually locked. My father took me round part of it once."

Jim turned away and was staring out of a small window

which allowed a beam of sunlight to light the sober place.

"You're right, of course."

Mary looked over his shoulder: from the window they could see a corner of the gardens and the stark wall of the tower wing.

"I'm hungry," Andrew said suddenly. He was tired of being inside the castle, however historic. "I'm sure it's past tea-time."

Katrine smiled and arm linked in Mary's, walked back to the more cheerful part of the castle.

"I must come again," she said. "I've got to explore the tower. I want to find the Room of the Mirror."

Mary stared. "But surely you don't believe that old legend?"

"Not really, no, but I want to find out about it. Father would never let me really explore. Sometimes I think that . . ."

"That what?" Mary felt a little afraid.

"Oh, nothing. It's time we got home, I suppose."

As they found their way towards the kitchen again and out, Mary tried to tell herself that she wasn't nervous, that the great place was just full of history and nothing more, but, looking at her friend's serious face, she was not sure.

As they got outside Jim waited to push the window to again.

"Gosh, it's good to be in the open air, again," he remarked. "You may be lucky to own such a place, Katrine, but it's pretty formidable, isn't it?"

Katrine looked at him then nodded.

"Yes. Yes, I suppose it is," she said softly.

CHAPTER SIX

THE WATCHER IN THE GLEN

THEY ALL crossed the courtyard and moved to the front of the castle without speaking.

Certainly Andrew whistled, staring around him, but even he said nothing.

Although the sun shone and the park was alive with wild things the reverse of sinister, from a merry grey squirrel racing up and down an elm, to a shy deer watching them from a thicket, Mary at least felt oppressed.

They reached the drive and turned to look back at the line of windows and at the grey tower beyond.

"A place like that wants living in," Jim said. "Pretty overwhelming otherwise."

Katrine agreed. She spoke dreamily.

"Father had fifteen guests over for the Twelfth last year and lots of people all summer."

"What kind of people?" asked Andrew.

"Oh, friends of his, Aunt Enid and some of her friends. He—he always said that the only excuse for having such a big place was to keep open house. In early summer we usually have children from the poor parts of Glasgow and Edinburgh."

"Hats off to you. Your father seems to have been quite a guy."

She flushed. "How I hate American expressions."

"I say, I am sorry." Jim spoke sincerely. Perhaps he, like Mary, found it difficult to credit that the owner of this fine place, who was also Katrine's father, was almost certainly dead.

They had turned off the drive now and were walking back by the way they had come. The lodge, Mary noticed, was still deserted.

Katrine, walking ahead, came back and took her arm.

"I wish I knew what had happened to the Nicholsons," she said. "I must explore the tower, I really must."

Jim sauntered by their sides. "Why?" he asked, adding: "I'm not being just curious, I really think we ought to know why you have come here. After all it must be hard for you, and what can you do?"

Katrine threw her head back. "I've come because I just cannot believe that Father is dead. I can't. He was an excellent swimmer, he knew every glen, every burn and hill like the palm of his hand. If he is dead . . ." she choked a little, "it's foul play."

Both Mary and Jim digested this in silence. Then Jim said, "I can guess how you feel, I'd be just the same. But what can you do alone? The police have investigated, naturally; it's three weeks ago, isn't it? What can you do?"

"I can find out what happened to him, and somehow, don't ask me why, I feel that it's got to do with the tower and the legend of the tower."

As she spoke Katrine was climbing ahead up the steep sides of the glen.

Jim leapt up and caught her arm.

"But this is nuts, an old story, what can it have to do with your father's disappearance?"

"I don't know. All I do know is that there is danger there, always has been—he would never allow me to explore it. Why, the only time I remember him being really angry with me—quite fierce, was when I was about ten and got in and began to climb down those steps."

Mary spoke suddenly. "Katrine, surely there is someone here in charge of the estate?"

"Of course, the factor, Ronald Besant is his name. He was partly disabled in the war, in the R.A.F., and Father gave him the job. He's very good."

"But where is he then?"

"Oh, he wouldn't live at the castle, though he used to come when we had people, of course. He's got a house at Glenavar over the hills."

"Why not go to him?" asked Jim.

"He's the last person I want to go to. Don't you understand? He mustn't know I'm here."

"But why?"

"He was Father's greatest friend. He'd be sure to send me back."

"Has he got a moustache?" asked Mary.

"No, he's clean-shaven, why?"

"I was thinking of the man I saw in the grounds last night."

"And he had a moustache?"

"Yes, I told you."

They were about to say more when Andrew, who had been running ahead, circled back and came rushing up.

"I say, see that little wood on the hillside?"

They stared in the direction of his waving arm.

"The larch wood. What's the matter?" asked Katrine.

"Someone was there, watching us. If you hadn't been yapping so much you'd have noticed. I think he's been kind of tracking us since we left the castle."

"Did you see him properly?" asked Jim.

"Only a glimpse—he was tall and thinnish and he was using binoculars. I think he knew I'd spotted him and skedaddled."

Katrine and Mary exchanged glances: could it be the stranger of last night?

"Let's get on," said Jim. "It's getting on for six."

The climb up was tiring and they were all glad when

they had clambered down on the other side and found the loch road below them and the roofs of The Old Manse comfortably near.

Looking at it as it stood beyond its garden in the sunshine, Mary felt her spirits rise again. This was home, that was the wonderful part of it, their new home, and to her, already home in the truest sense of the word.

Mrs. Carew was in the garden taking a breath of air after a busy day. She welcomed them all in relief.

"My word, you've been a time, dears," she said, "and how hot and tired you look. Never mind we'll have a high tea to-day, I know you'll be ready for it."

Andrew was staring anxiously round.

"Where's Boodle?"

His mother laughed. "I've persuaded Lilian to sit down and rest for a while. Boodle is on her knee."

He dashed ahead of them into the house.

In the big hall stood a large, rather shabby, case. "Not a visitor already?" cried Jim.

"Yes, Jim." His mother seemed pleased. "Mr. Canning came in this afternoon just after you had left. I showed him that room on the first floor and he's taken it. But he won't be coming in to-day after all."

"Why?"

"He made a telephone call, to Edinburgh I think, half an hour after he had come and said he would have to leave his case and return to-morrow."

"What an odd kind of visitor," said Mary, "what was he like?"

"Oh, ordinary, quite pleasant, wants to get some fishing. He wrote his name in the visitors' book, by the way."

Mary had the curiosity to go and look at the brand-new visitors' book which lay ready in the small room off the dining-room which would be used as an office.

"George Canning, London," was written in a long sloping hand.

They all washed and changed, then came down to high tea. It was a good tea with fresh cold salmon from some burn, left by the ubiquitous Jamie Ferguson, salad, jam and bread and cake; a high tea to end all high teas as Jim put it.

They had finished and the two girls were clearing and doing the washing up, when Lilian came in to tell Katrine that there was a telephone call for her.

"Hurry, my dear, it's long distance," she said. Katrine looked astonished, hurriedly wiped her hands and went into the hall to take it. She was away some time and, when she got back, she was looking bewildered.

"That was Aunt Enid, Mary," she explained. "Funny, but I always had the idea that she is so busy with her lectures and work and so on, that she scarcely realised where I was."

"You didn't want her to, did you?"

"No, though of course I showed her your mother's letter. Anyhow she must have noted the address all right for I haven't had time to write to her yet. Mary!"

"Yes?"

"She has had extraordinary news. Remember me telling you that we had scarcely any relations at all except for some who are abroad. Well, it seems that my father's cousin and his wife have turned up from New Zealand."

"Your father's cousin?"

"Yes. His uncle, Angus Maclure, was killed in the war and this is his son. But he never bothered to write or anything before."

"But he'll be your aunt's cousin, too?" Mary was becoming a little confused.

"Only by marriage. Aunt Enid was my mother's sister. Mother died soon after I was born."

"I see. Well, perhaps you'll like them. At least they are relations."

"I don't know, I don't know at all. Father never spoke of them, and after all they never wrote or anything. But Aunt Enid says they are touring in a car and will be coming up here next week. I ought really to ask your mother to keep a room for them." Katrine spoke without enthusiasm, and Mary was not surprised. After all, as Katrine had said, they had never troubled to keep up with her or her father through the years.

However she told Mary's mother, who promised to keep them a room.

"We don't know yet whether the colonel and his wife and old Mrs. Hammond are coming, and, if they do, it will not be until next week, thank goodness."

"Don't you like the idea of guests after all, Mummy?" asked Mary anxiously.

"Of course I do, the more the merrier, but I'm grateful for the time to get everything in real order. There's still a lot to do."

The rest of the day passed without incident. They were all tired and went to bed early.

Mary lay awake a long time, staring out at the fading gold of the sky. She was thinking of the castle, of its beauty, its remoteness, and trying to place Katrine as the owner of all that. She felt sad about her, although she understood how she must feel. For her father to disappear like that, not to know what had happened, was very, very hard. But this talk of the tower, of the Room with the Mirror, of some dread secret which it concealed, was pure fantasy. Jim had thought so too, and, knowing Jim, she realised that the whole business made him very uneasy.

What could she do? She remembered the phone message Katrine had received, and hoped that these new cousins would be nice and perhaps reason with her as *they* could not—but all the same she was doubtful. The Carews had cousins, a whole lot of them, but they rarely heard from them, save at Christmas when they exchanged cards and presents. No, Katrine was very much alone, that was the trouble.

She heard the door next to hers being closed softly and smiled sleepily. Andrew, no doubt, had gone down and brought up his kitten.

Rather to Mary's surprise, next day Katrine made no mention of the castle, or a return visit to it, only threw herself whole-heartedly into helping about the house. She looked almost happy when arranging books, or helping unpack ornaments and the rest of the china, in being busy in a purely domestic way.

When Lilian showed her how to make bannocks she watched her intently, head on one side.

"I love cooking," she confessed, "but I never had a chance of trying my hand at it."

Watching her, Mary wondered about her life at the castle. Deserted now, it had obviously been well kept up. There must have been quite a staff of servants. Thinking of this she said, "Katrine, you must have had lots of help in the castle. Where are they now?"

"Dad's old batman, O'Reilly and his wife managed, with the help of three people from the village. As it happened Daddy meant to come up to London in July so he let them have their holiday now. They're in Ireland with a married son. O'Reilly was very upset when— when it happened, he wrote to me."

"How funny to have Irish servants."

"Perhaps, but Pat O'Reilly saved my father's life at Alamein, and he was devoted to him."

Mary was annoyed with herself. "I should keep my silly tongue still," she thought, as she noticed the old sadness on her friend's face again.

That afternoon the two boys went down to the loch, and, finding an old boat there, began to row a little by the shores. Jim rowed well, but Andrew caught a crab more than once, and although they asked the girls to come with them, they were not tempted.

"Suppose we go into the village," said Katrine. "Ask your mother if she wants anything."

Consequently at three o'clock, clad in slacks and thin pullovers, for the sun was warm, they took the winding road to the village.

Katrine was rather quiet and Mary chatted of their plans for the Manse, of school, of mutual friends, of anything which would take the other's mind off her strange quest.

Once in the village Katrine's reception there was almost royal. Her presence seemed to go from mouth to mouth, and people hurried out of cottages, speaking to her in the courteous way the Scots have.

A little old woman came hurrying up.

"Katrine Maclure, it is. Eh, dearie, dinna greet, the Maclure was a fine man and weel missed."

An elderly man stopped them as they went into the post office-cum-general store and held out his hand.

"'Tis guid tae see ye, Miss Maclure! Gin ye feel on yer ain, ye've friends leal and true here."

The McCalls who kept the post office were tactfully kind.

"'Tis fine to have ye back, Miss Katrine," said tall, sandy-haired Mrs. McCall. "And ye're at The Old Manse? Yin of the leddies, I hear telt, is Scottish, and the other a bonnie one and kind."

Katrine was touched, Mary knew, almost to tears, and,

when they had made their few purchases, Katrine left, a proud look on her face, trying hard not to break down.

"What lovely people they are," Mary said as they turned homewards. "It must be good to be liked like that."

"When I'm older I'll do all I can for them. There's quite a bit of poverty here, you know. We always try to help," she added faintly.

"Of course." Mary knew she was thinking of her father. Most of the villagers, with the tact of their kind, had not mentioned his strange disappearance but it might well be that Katrine was the last of the Maclures.

When they reached home they found a long, low, red sports car in the drive. Remembering the man Canning, Mary wondered if it were his car, until she noticed Katrine's face.

Katrine held her arm.

"It's Ronald," she said, "I wonder how he found out I'm here. Stay with me, Mary."

She seemed so upset that Mary expected someone formidable waiting to see them.

Instead they found her mother entertaining a tall, fair man with a delicate-looking aquiline face which reminded her somewhat of the late Leslie Howard.

He rose when the two girls entered and came forward. He used a stick and limped, and Mary remembered what Katrine had said about his being injured in the R.A.F.

"Hallo, Katrine," he said pleasantly, "this will be Mary, I know."

"How did you know I was here?" asked Katrine, and her manner was a little hostile.

"Oh, things get round, you know." They sat and Mrs. Carew excused herself, glancing at Mary. But Mary stayed as Katrine had asked her.

They were silent a moment then Ronald Besant spoke

gently. "You shouldn't have come, my dear. It is no use making yourself unhappy."

"I had to come. Ronald, I've got to find out."

"Find out what?"

"About my father."

He shook his head. "Katrine, I was very fond of your father. Believe me, everything has been done to find him. I racked my brains for a reason and explanation—nothing. What can *you* do?"

"I don't know." She stood up, "Don't tell Mrs. Carew to send me away, Ronald, please!"

"Why should I do that? I'm glad you have found friends, though sorry it is here." He looked at Mary. "You're quite a family, I believe. I hope you'll keep your impetuous friend well guarded."

"Guarded?"

He shrugged. "Well, don't let her do anything impetuous."

Katrine had relaxed and she seemed relieved.

"Ronald," she said, "what has happened to the Nicholsons?"

"Nothing, they'll be back in a week. They went to stay with their son and his family in London. Why, you haven't been to the castle, have you?"

"We all went," said Mary.

Katrine nodded. "And I must go again. Ronald, I want to examine the tower."

He frowned. "The tower, why?"

"Only—I don't really know, intuition perhaps, but I feel there's a clue to Father's disappearance there," she paused, "will you come?"

"No." The one word was very definite. "It's an uncanny place at best, and I believe it isn't at all safe."

"Did the police, and the other people looking for Father go into it?"

"I don't know, I don't think so." He stood up. "Now, Katrine, you must stop this nonsense. I know it's all terribly tough, I know how you must feel, you poor child, but leave the castle, and most certainly the tower, alone. You must realise that everything is being done, is, remember, *still* being done to find your father. Try and be content to stay here with your friends and make no attempt to interfere."

Katrine seemed to be trying to digest this, then she said, "Perhaps the Ian Maclures will want to see it. They'll certainly want to go over the castle."

Ronald Besant dropped his stick, stooped to pick it up and asked, "What is this about the Ian Maclures? I thought they were on the other side of the world, Australia, isn't it?"

"New Zealand. No, they're in England, they got in touch with Aunt Enid. They're on tour and coming up here next week."

Abruptly he got to his feet and limped across the room, standing a moment to look out of the window towards the loch and the distant castle.

"Let me see, Ian Maclure will be the son of Angus, your father's uncle, who was killed in the war?"

"Yes, we've never met, of course."

"Now I wonder . . ." he spoke thoughtfully.

"What?"

"If they've heard of what has happened."

"I don't know," Katrine spoke tonelessly.

"Well, I must go now. Now don't do anything rash, Katrine. Remember wiser heads than yours are busy on the problem." He smiled at Mary. "Take care of her, she's worth it."

They walked with him to his car and watched him turn it and drive swiftly away.

"He's nice," remarked Mary, "I like him. Why didn't you want to see him?"

"I like him very much myself but I thought he might come the heavy hand on me and force me to leave." She smiled, her serious face lighting up, "I know he liked you all. I'm so glad. But Mary, don't you see?"

"See what?"

"He's as puzzled and shocked as I am about—about everything. Even he, who knew him so well, can't understand how and why Father disappeared. But they're still investigating everything."

Mary had nothing to say, for she was afraid to encourage her friend to hope too much.

CHAPTER SEVEN

A SHOCK FOR KATRINE

BY THE WEEK-END, after the family, including Katrine, had worked hard arranging the rooms, checking linen, china and cutlery, making provisional lists of what would be needed for their future guests, they were able to relax at last and decide that all was ready.

The young people had kept near home, although Jim had given them a row over the loch, having taken possession of a rather heavy boat which Murdo the boatman had told them belonged to the Manse.

"As a matter of fact I think it's one of his. He's just being decent," Jim remarked. "And they talk about the Scots being mean!"

By this time they had all met the big, red-headed Murdo and his son, who had charge of the small boathouse not far from the Manse. It was literally a boathouse, as they lived over it, in three sparsely furnished, very clean little rooms. Murdo made a living in hiring out his boats to tourists and he also fished—for trout, in the burn which came down from the hills and fed the loch, also for occasional salmon, as well as dace and the more common fresh-water fish.

It was on the Saturday that they received a letter from Colonel Brayne accepting their terms and saying that they would be coming over that Monday. Mrs. Hamilton had not yet replied, and the suitcase belonging to the man who had signed himself George Canning, still stood in a corner, for he had not returned.

Mrs. Carew was puzzled.

"I can't understand it. After all he left his case, saw the room, telephoned, then said that he would be returning the next day. What can have become of him?"

"I shouldn't worry, Mum, he's left his suitcase here, so he's bound to turn up," said Jim.

His mother was worrying, but about something different. "I'm wondering if it is at all possible to get into Perth to-day," she said, after they had discussed the colonel and his lady's arrival over breakfast. "Quite frankly we haven't enough china. I need another dinner service and a tea service, too."

"Good," cried Andrew, "I hate that old white stuff we're making do with."

Lilian looked thoughtful. "I wonder, would Ferguson run us in? Katrine, where is a good, not expensive place to get china?"

"There's Dickie's. They have lovely stuff. Like me to come, too?"

"Why, yes, dear. You do know Perth. But we don't want lovely stuff, we need hard-wearing, ordinary china —but not too plain."

Katrine brightened. "Good, let's ring Ferguson. I know Perth well and you can lunch with me."

"Dutch treat if you like, my dear."

"Please!"

Mrs. Carew shook her head. By this time she knew that Katrine was generous to a fault.

Seeing Katrine, Mother and Lilian off at ten-thirty that morning, Mary tried not to be disappointed. After all someone had to be left in charge, and she and Jim could cope easily enough.

Once they had gone in fact she felt rather responsible and pleased. As their elders had hurried off, there was a good deal of dusting and tidying-up to be done in the house, and she got busy, having sent the boys into the garden to see if there were any potatoes to be dug up.

There were and she was called to admire the harvest, even taking a spade herself. It was rather fun, she found, to dig deep and come upon a little nest of large tubers. A fat and cheerful bird came and hopped round looking for worms, and a couple of squirrels ran about in the trees beyond.

Now and then they heard the sound of cars on the loch road. The season for holidays had begun and quite a few tourists found their way there.

"I hope Murdo lets lots of boats to-day," Andrew was saying, as Jim suddenly turned to Mary.

"I say, isn't that the phone? We shouldn't all have left the house."

That was true. Mary threw down her spade and ran. She rushed into the hall. The phone was ringing, and just as she reached it, it stopped. She took up the receiver, no sound. She had been just too late.

Jim had followed her.

"Missed it. I say, what a bind. We should have remembered that one of us should stay in."

It was no use worrying. They could only hope that the caller would try again.

Mary went into the kitchen to make the lunch. They would have egg and chips, she decided, and began to peel potatoes, some of their own potatoes, lovely thought! She was doing this when the phone rang again.

This time she was in the hall within half a minute and snatched up the receiver.

"That The Old Manse, Lendaloch?"

"Speaking. I mean, yes." Mary almost giggled.

"Canning here. Sorry I couldn't make it yesterday, I was delayed. I shall be coming on this evening. About six."

"Yes. Thank you for telling us. We shall expect you."

"Thank you. Good-bye."

The voice had been pleasant enough, rather low in tone. Putting back the receiver, Mary thought she had heard that kind of voice before, though she could not remember when.

"It was the Canning man," she explained to her two brothers who had come in and were waiting curiously.

"What did he sound like?"

"All right. Very polite." She giggled. "He said, ' Is that The Old Manse? ' and I answered, ' Speaking.'"

They all laughed, for it struck them as being irresistibly funny.

The pleasant old house seemed very quiet without their elders and Katrine, and, after lunching and washing up, Jim was restless. Andrew was playing with his kitten on the lawn.

"What are you going to do this afternoon?" asked Mary.

"I was thinking of trying out young Andrew's fishing-rod in the burn, but it's some way off. Don't like leaving you here on your own."

"Don't be silly. I shall be all right. Look, I'll bring out one of those old deck-chairs and sit on the lawn. I've got quite a lot of holiday reading to do—Shakespeare for my School Cert. I ought to try and get some done before we get too busy."

"You're sure you'll be all right?"

"Of course. And I can hear the phone if I leave the front door open. All right, indeed!"

Andrew came charging up. "Did you say something about fishing?" he asked.

In the end Mary saw them off burdened with the rod, and, optimistically, an ancient creel they had found in the house, and went to get her chair and books.

She arranged the chair strategically within sound of the open door and in the shade of some bushes, then lay back, books as yet unopened.

How quiet it was. The birds seemed to be having their afternoon sleep, although occasionally there was a quacking from a flotilla of ducks which haunted the loch near Murdo's headquarters, and a rustle from the woods when a little breeze rose and fell.

Once she heard the sound of a launch chugging away on the distant water, the occasional whirr of a car passing, that was all.

She opened her book, a copy of *The Tempest* with notes, and began to read without, it must be said, much concentration.

After a while she glanced up uneasily and stared at the shrubbery on her left which cut off the side of the kitchen garden. She had a feeling that she was being watched by something more formidable than a bright-eyed squirrel.

Imagination, of course. She tried to go on reading. Then abruptly she heard the crackle of a foot on some twigs and stood up, her book falling to the grass.

Someone was coming through the orchard, his feet crackling on leaves and fallen twigs. A moment later he appeared from the shrubbery, a big man, tall and with a military look. He had sandy hair and a moustache. The man she had encountered her first night here?

He approached her quickly.

"I hope I haven't startled you."

It was the same man, she would have known that pleasant, faintly Scottish voice anywhere.

"Well, you did," she managed.

"I'm sorry. You all alone?"

"My brothers will be back at any time now."

He smiled. "Good, I must meet them." He glanced at

the vacant garden chair. "Sit down again, do, I only want a short word with you."

Mechanically she sat and he threw himself down on the grass not far from her, and looked at her with interest.

"Katrine Maclure is staying with you, isn't she?"

"Yes, she's at school with me, as a matter of fact."

"I'd like a talk with her." He studied her, his eyes were blue and bright and very shrewd. "Must do one of these days. Tell me, how is she taking her father's disappearance?"

"She's very unhappy. She came here to try and help."

"And can she?"

"I don't see how. It's all rather dreadful really."

"She talks to you, of course. Has she any clue to her father's going like this?"

"No, not one. But . . ."

"Yes?"

"She's got an idea that it's something to do with the legend."

"The legend?"

"Of the Maclure's disappearing, one every third generation, something like that. She hasn't said so in so many words, but I know she thinks it's something to do with the tower."

He said nothing then he gave her one of his quick direct glances. "You're fond of her?"

"Yes, of course."

"Well, I shouldn't encourage her to try and do anything. If she goes to the castle, go with her, and definitely discourage her from exploring the tower. It's unsafe and some of these legends arise from something perhaps purely physical. Understand?"

"Yes, I do. Jim said that."

"Jim?"

"My brother. Only . . ." she hesitated for a moment.

"Yes?"

"Katrine wants to explore the tower."

"Don't let her. It's an uncanny place at best, and not safe."

Mary was quiet, then she asked, "Who are you?"

He rose to his considerable height.

"The name is MacShane. I'm investigating the Maclure's disappearance. At present I don't need or want to worry his daughter, but quite frankly I'm uneasy about her being here."

"But why? Because of the legend?"

"The legend? Perhaps, as I said just now, some places get an uncanny name for no reason, but often there is a real reason behind it. People make up a legend, yes, but it is founded on fact which may have started it all. Follow me?"

"I think so."

He looked at the pleasant house, the quiet garden, then at her. "And I shouldn't mention this little talk to Katrine Maclure."

"Why?"

"Because, my dear, it might give her false hope. Her father may be alive, but it's nearly a month now."

"I know." Mary spoke unhappily.

"In fact," he went on, "perhaps it would be as well if you kept this little talk of ours entirely to yourself."

"Why?"

"Shall we say, I have my reasons," he smiled suddenly, then raised his hand in salute and strode quickly away down the drive to the road.

A detective! In a way Mary felt reassured. At least it showed that, as Ronald Besant had said, the search was still going on.

She had liked him, and yet she had felt that he was

far from optimistic about the result of his investigations. A month is a long time.

But why had he been so definite about warning her about the tower? He was certainly not the type to believe in legends and family curses. The place was unsafe, probably as he had hinted, it came to that.

She wished, all the same, that he had not made her promise to keep their talk secret. She would have liked to tell Jim all about it and get his opinion.

However, when the boys came racing up with three somewhat pathetic specimens of fish they had caught, she did not mention her visitor. Not that she wasn't tempted to do so, but, no doubt the detective had had good reason for his request.

Consequently, she let the boys tease her about her alleged laziness, lying with a book unopened on her knee, and said nothing, only went in to make the tea.

Their mother rang up at about four to say that they would not be in until about seven.

"We've got some nice china, not at all expensive, and Katrine wanted to see a film, so we're just going in. Ferguson is being very kind and waiting for us."

"Good, Mummy. I'll get something nice for your meal."

"Do, darling. Any news?"

"Oh, yes, the Canning man is coming this evening about six."

"Oh dear! His room is ready. Remember to take in some hot water for him when he arrives, give him a cup of tea or anything he wants. I wish I'd known he was coming."

Mary reassured her, then went to cut more bread and butter for Andrew, who always ate a huge tea.

When the meal was over she went upstairs and gave the guest's room a quick dust, made up the bed with the linen and blankets already there, and, as an afterthought, put some flowers in a vase on the bedside table, to give a good impression, as she told herself.

After that there was only the evening meal to plan and partly prepare.

She was peeling potatoes and cutting cabbage, having decided that the mince they had in hand would make a suitable evening meal, when she heard the sound of a car. It was only half-past five. Their guest was early. She found Jim and Andrew in the hall. They were staring out at the small blue Ford which had just driven up.

Mary stared with them. A slight, dark man was getting out. He was hatless and his receding dark hair showed above a narrow face lit by a pair of brown eyes.

They all turned and looked at one another.

"That's the man in the train," cried Andrew, "the one who asked us the time."

Mary's heart sank. She felt so shocked that, when he appeared in the doorway, it took her all her courage to greet him appropriately.

He smiled around at them. "Well, well, surely we've met before?"

Jim answered lightly.

"Yes, you were on the train with us on Wednesday."

"Of course, I remember now, I asked you the time." He looked round brightly, "I know I'm early, I'll go up for a wash, I think."

"Would you like some tea? We dine at seven," said Mary.

"That would be very nice." He was staring at her in some surprise.

"My mother is out. She went to Perth but she'll be back for supper."

"Good. Have you many guests?"

"No. We have only just come here as a matter of fact."

"Just yourselves," he glanced at Andrew and Jim, "and your mother."

"And Lilian," added Andrew. "She's mother's partner."

The man smiled, showing excellent teeth which gave him the appearance of a super-intelligent fox, then followed Jim, who carried his bag upstairs.

Mary never knew how she got through the next hour. This was the man whom Katrine had seen in the school grounds, who had followed her in the train, and caused her to leave it at Carlisle. Somehow she must warn her in good time, before she reached the house.

She gave the new guest tea, cake, and bread and butter, and smiled at his pleasant thanks—"What an efficient young lady you are"—then went into the kitchen to talk to the boys.

Jim agreed with her that Katrine must be warned. "I'll go up to the corner and stop the car before it gets here," he suggested.

"No, I'd better go. I'll make some excuse to ask Katrine to get out. Mother will have to be told later."

"Let me go," pleaded Andrew.

"Look here, young Andrew," said his brother, "be careful with this Canning character. He mustn't guess that Katrine is here with us."

"But what is she going to do then?" asked the boy.

What indeed? They couldn't very well keep her concealed in the house all the time, though she might stay in the upper rooms. Mary felt most terribly depressed, for it looked as though Katrine would not be able to stay with them any longer.

She was at the bend of the road by half-past six waiting for Ferguson's old shooting brake. She waited for a good half-hour before she saw it coming and dashed into the road, hand out.

D

They all looked very happy. Mother was gay, and Lilian, hugging parcels, looked pleased.

Katrine too was bright. "Hallo, what is it?" she asked.

"Anything the matter?" Mother was suddenly worried.

"Nothing really, Mum, but could Katrine get out and walk with me? I want to tell her something."

Mother looked surprised, as well she might.

"Please, Mummy, it *is* important. I'll tell you afterwards. And the man has arrived."

Katrine was already climbing out; something in Mary's face had told her that this was important.

They both waited until the car had disappeared round the bend, then Mary took Katrine's arm and drew her to a little copse of trees over by the loch.

"The man Canning who has just arrived! Katrine, he's the man who followed you on the train."

Katrine paled. "Are you sure?"

"Yes, quite. He knew us, said as much. Katrine, what does it mean, are you certain he really followed you?"

"Quite certain. Mary, I shan't be able to stay with you any longer."

"But where can you go?"

The other stared across the loch to where the old grey tower of the castle showed above the heat haze beyond the still blue waters.

"I'll go to the castle"—she laughed wryly—"plenty of room there."

Mary was thinking of blue eyes in a thin shrewd face, remembering MacShane's warning.

"But you can't. You mustn't."

"Why? It may be a good thing in a way. I'm convinced that there's something there which will give me the clue I'm after."

"Please, Katrine, don't go there! What about Mr. Besant, wouldn't he put you up?"

"I suppose so. But no, this is the best plan. I'll go to the castle."

"Not to-night."

"Why not?"

"Well you'll want food, provisions, blankets and everything. It's just impossible."

"I suppose so."

Mary was thinking quickly. "Look, I'll go back now and see where that man is. You'll have to come in by the back way and stay there for the time being, then go up to your room."

"My room is on the same landing as his, I saw your mother preparing it."

"I know what I'll do; I'll take some bedding up to the garret."

Finally Mary hurried off, found Jim and sent him back to be with Katrine, a thing he seemed most willing to do.

As she turned into the kitchen, hoping to find her mother, she came to a decision. If Katrine insisted on going to stay at the castle she would go with her—certainly at night when she would not be needed at home.

Katrine could not stay alone at the castle, she was convinced of that.

CHAPTER EIGHT

IN THE CASTLE

ONCE IN the house Mary found that Mr. Canning was now installed in the lounge. Her mother was talking to him, so she went up to Katrine's room and began to take clothes off the bed.

Selecting a room on the top floor, a room with a sloping ceiling, she remade the bed there; then, because it would be as well if Katrine was not seen on any other floor, she quickly packed her clothes, toilet articles also, and took them up.

Then, hurrying into the kitchen she sent Andrew, who was enjoying what he considered to be a promising adventure, to go and tell Jim and Katrine that the coast was clear and to come round by the back.

Her mother came in at that moment and overheard her. "What *is* the matter, Mary?"

She told her, finishing with, "And we can't let this man know she is here."

Mrs. Carew shook her head. "But why should this man, who seems all right—he tells me he works in a bank in London, and is touring the Highlands—follow Katrine? I can't help feeling that the shock of her father's death has made her over-nervous, poor child!"

"But he has followed her!"

"But, my dear, why should he? And even if he has, she'll be safe enough with us under our own roof. Anyhow where would she go?"

"That's what I don't like, Mummy. She wants to go and stay in the castle."

"That huge pile! Well, I wouldn't like it, I'd be terrified, living in a huge place with so many rooms and an eerie name." She broke off as Jim came in with Katrine.

Katrine looked flushed and excited.

"Is it safe here?" she asked.

"Of course."

Jim turned to Andrew. "Go into the lounge, old boy, and tell us if the Canning character is likely to stray in here."

Their mother laughed.

"Really, aren't you all making too much of this?"

Katrine spoke seriously.

"I'm not, truly, Mrs. Carew." She paused, "Where is your friend?"

"Lilian is in the garden picking raspberries. Your job, Andrew, by the way."

Katrine perched on the big table. "This man was watching me at the school towards the end of term. He was on the train to Perth. You see, I know that there was something, something very sinister, behind my father's disappearance. Perhaps, whoever was behind it, wants to keep an eye on me. I don't know, but he mustn't know I'm here, he mustn't!"

Mother looked thoughtful and worried.

"I can only think then that the best thing for you to do would be to go back to your aunt."

"It is the last thing I shall do," said Katrine firmly. "Anyhow, once in the castle, I shall be able to look round. Really investigate."

Mrs. Carew was obstinate. "In a way I'm in charge of you now, and responsible. You mustn't go to that great place alone."

"But I'm going with her," Mary spoke triumphantly. "She'll sleep here to-night up in the garret part; I've done her room, and we'll start out to-morrow morning. I'll come back to give a hand in the day, Mum, I really will, and one of the boys can be with her when I'm away, but I'll sleep there at night."

"I can too," said Jim.

Mrs. Carew was still worried. "I don't like it at all," she said. "Why don't you get in touch with that nice Mr. Besant; he would advise you."

Katrine felt she had won her point. "I shall. And don't you see if Mary or Jim or Andrew are always with me at the castle, I shan't be alone."

Lilian came in at the moment and the discussion ended. No doubt Mother would tell her everything later on—as it was, the meal had to be prepared.

Mr. Canning was served dinner in solitude in the dining-room and the family took theirs in the small room off the kitchen which would be their own private sitting-room from now on. Whilst they ate, their mother was very quiet. It was obvious that she was thinking over the whole business and not liking it. After supper, Katrine, saying she was tired, excused herself and went up to her new room. Mary followed her up.

"You're an angel, it looks really nice. But before I go to bed I must pack. I only want a few odds and ends, a change of linen, slacks and so on. We can start early to-morrow for the castle and I'll get installed there."

It was Mary's turn to feel doubtful.

"I can't help feeling Mum is right, Katrine. It's such a huge place. Why not stay here? You can always get out when that man is away; he won't hang round the house all day."

"No. Sooner or later he'd be bound to see me."

"What will you do about food?"

"I'll have to rely on you for that. I'm not even sure the water and heat is on. But we'll manage." She laughed suddenly. "It'll be fun, you'll see. I shall never be alone, one of you will be with me, and you'll stay the night."

"I promise to do that."

"And I know exactly where we'll make our head-quarters—in the west wing farthest from the tower. There are two bedrooms and a sitting-room all on one floor. It was used by my grandfather when he was old and ill. It's the very place."

"The farther away from the tower the better," said Mary with feeling.

She had left Katrine in her new room and was coming down to the lower floor when Jim appeared and drew her into his room.

"Everything O.K.?" he asked.

She nodded.

"I've been thinking," he went on. "Agreed that she can't be left at the castle alone. One of us can stand by in the day. You're going to sleep there, too?"

"That's the idea."

"I think I'd better come as well. You need a man to stand by." Jim drew himself up to his considerable height. "May be nothing in all this, but on the other hand there may. Will Katrine mind, do you think?"

"She'll be delighted. What's the plan for to-morrow?"

"We're getting up early, and we'll row across to the castle and get installed there. You could come over—say, at about nine, and relieve me, for I've just got to do my bit here."

"What about food, and all that?"

"We'll have breakfast first, then see what's needed. After all we've the whole day to go over to the castle and back."

Jim's face was set and he had a look Mary knew well. He had looked like this when he went in to bat for his school last term and almost got his century. "Do you know, I rather think this is going to be quite interesting," was all he said.

Next morning Mary sat in the bows of the old rowing-boat next to Katrine, who had the ropes, as Jim sculled them across the still, deep water towards the castle.

It was a most beautiful day. Haze lay on the heights, Benavar's beautiful head was wreathed in mist, birds circled over the water, and, so early was it, scarcely six, that no human stirred.

Katrine had been up at five-thirty, and they had had a breakfast of eggs, bacon and fried bread before starting.

Andrew they had left sleeping, and both the girls, certainly Katrine, had been surprised when Jim appeared in the kitchen when they were cooking the meal, fully dressed.

"I'll take you across," he had announced calmly. They were only too glad of his help. Mary had made Katrine pack sheets and a couple of blankets in an old case as well as her own clothes. She had wanted to add provisions but Katrine had refused.

"I'd rather get in some from the village. Perhaps Andrew could get them and bring them over." She had put, in the lavish way she had, a five pound note in a cannister on the dresser.

Now they were on their way.

As they neared the farther shore, Katrine directed Jim along the rushy bank towards a little landing-stage. It lay at the foot of the castle grounds and beyond was a boat-house, its doors padlocked.

A small path led upwards towards the back of the castle and leaving Jim to fasten the boat, they hurried along this and round to the courtyard.

It was absolutely deserted, and the window they had forced was as they had left it and it opened with ease. In the bright sunlight they had all felt quite optimistic, even cheerful, but, once in the dimmish passage inside the great place, the silence was oppressive.

Perhaps realising this, Katrine hurried to the front, then up the wide stairs and along a corridor which went towards the west wing.

Brother and sister followed in silence. It was so very big. Mary stifled the thought of how big and silent it would be when night fell.

But Katrine had opened a wide door, crossed a room and pulled curtains. Following her, they found themselves in a large, almost circular room, where there were easy-chairs, books on shelves by the hearth, and, in one corner, an invalid chair. It was a cheerful place, once the light had been allowed to filter in, with its panelled walls offset by gay, green and yellow curtains.

"My boudoir," laughed Katrine, as she opened another door which gave off this room, revealing a bedroom with a large comfortable bed, its mattress turned up, but otherwise furnished adequately.

"And here," she said, going out into the passage again, "is another bedroom. It was used by my grandfather's valet, but if Jim comes he won't mind."

Certainly it was smaller and a trifle gloomy, but the bed looked comfortable.

"We'll sleep together in the bigger room, if that's all right by you," went on Katrine.

Mary brightened. The arrangement seemed perfect. She and Katrine could share the room, Jim would be only a few feet away; the suite was in the new wing, farthest from the tower, as Katrine had explained before.

"Now, for the linen cupboard," said Katrine practically, and led the way out and along another corridor towards the main bedrooms of the castle. A large linen cupboard, which was a room in itself, lay off the big bathroom on that floor. On its shelves were linen, towels of every shape and size and colour, and blankets. Mary took them out experimentally, but they felt damp.

"They need airing," she said. "And I don't see how we're going to kindle a fire."

"Never mind, it's going to be a hot day," we'll put them all on a line in the courtyard," said Jim, as practical as his sister. "I'm sure I saw an attachment for one there."

Katrine was trying the taps in the bathroom: the water ran, which was something. They had already tried the electric lights but the current was off.

Finally they went down into the great kitchen. It was Jim who found rope in one of the huge dresser drawers, and he who fixed the line. Quite soon blankets, sheets and pillow-cases were flapping gently in the breeze.

Mary looked at them, frowning.

"Supposing someone sees them?"

Katrine looked up at the blank windows, at the empty stables, and garage.

"Who is there to see them?" she asked.

Time was passing but the two girls dusted and organised the sitting-room and bedrooms, the last only waiting for the beds to be made, and, at about nine, Mary became uneasy.

"Mummy will be wondering where we are," she said. "I should go back and help."

Jim looked at Katrine. "Mind being left half an hour?" he asked.

"Of course not. There are books and things, and I can toddle about the grounds," she laughed.

"Good, I'll take Mary over, then come back. After that Andrew can come for a bit." He paused. "You have a telephone?"

"Of course—in the main hall, and there are switches to other parts as well."

He was already hurrying down the main stairs. They

followed and watched him as he took up the receiver which stood on a large refectory table to one side of the great windows.

He put it back and turned. "It's O.K. That's fine, just fine. Anything up and you can ring us, or the police or anyone." Katrine looked relieved, too.

"That's marvellous. One's never quite alone with a phone to hand."

Jim sculled Mary across again, left her on the bank below the Manse and returned, leaving her to run to the house.

As she had expected, her mother was worried and annoyed. "Where have you been? To that castle, of course. You might have told me," she said.

Andrew, feeding his kitten, added: "Me, too. Mean of you."

"You know what Katrine's like," said Mary apologetically. "We've left her there, and arranged the rooms for her to stay, in the west wing. Jim will stay with her for a bit, then come back. Andrew, you can go over then."

"Goody," said Andrew, "reminds me of that old story about rowing over the fox and the chickens, you know."

Mary knew, but she was far too busy soothing her mother to think about the connection at the moment.

"How is our Mr. Canning?" she asked after a while.

"Having his breakfast. I must say he seems quite a pleasant man."

Lilian came in at that moment. When she saw Mary she looked relieved. "There you are, you wicked girl! Your mother's been quite worried."

"I came back to help. We've settled Katrine in her castle," she explained.

Lilian's kind face was troubled.

"It's all most odd. How on earth can she stay there all alone?" She paused, and then, "If we weren't so busy I'd go over," she added.

Mrs. Carew gave her a quick glance.

"Perhaps you could, dear. Go over and see what these terrible young people are up to. I can't leave here, I'm afraid. But we're practically to rights, with only one guest to see to until Monday. You go."

Mary hurried out to see if their guest had finished his breakfast yet.

He had and the table waited to be cleared. He stood at the window, staring out across the garden to the loch.

He turned when she came in.

"Good morning, my dear." He had very white and rather pointed teeth which showed when he smiled. "That's an odd old pile over there. Would it be the Castle of Lendaloch?"

"It would, I mean, yes it is."

"Well, well, I'm most interested in such ancient places. How does one get there?"

Mary went very still within herself.

"It's quite a climb all round the verge of the loch," she said, "then down on the other side. Miles and miles."

"But surely it is easiest to row across? Indeed I thought I saw a boat coming in half an hour ago."

"Yes, I was out with my brother."

"Good, perhaps he could row me across. This afternoon?"

Mary played for time. "I'm afraid not this afternoon. We're very busy you see."

She began to pile dishes on a tray and went out hurriedly.

It would not be long before he discovered Murdo and

his boats. She remembered the clothes on the line, the signs, all too evident, that someone was there. Katrine must be warned and as soon as possible.

She found Andrew and told him to keep an eye on the guest.

"But I want to go over to the castle and be with Katrine," he objected.

"You shall. But just watch him for a bit. Find out if he goes out and particularly if he discovers the boat-house."

"O.K."

Andrew clumped off.

In spite of her panic, the day passed quite without incident. In the afternoon Lilian took a basket with bread, butter, a Thermos of tea and other provisions, and got Murdo to row her across to the castle with Andrew.

Not long after this Jim returned, hungry and quite pleased with life.

"Katrine and I had a busy morning. She showed me all over the castle," he said. "Some place it is too! Then we walked in the grounds and looked at the greenhouses. Katrine thinks that the caretakers will soon be back, because they've left the heat on and the tomatoes are coming on fine there. We all but ran into an old chap who was doing a bit of gardening too, so it isn't as absolutely deserted as you'd think."

Mr. Canning seemed to have contented himself with a very restful day. Most of the time he sat in the garden, and he did not attempt to go down the road.

He ate his lunch and asked about the fishing like any other visitor; certainly he did not mention the castle again.

Lilian returned by six, full of talk about the castle, which she had known as a girl but never entered.

"It's a wonderful place, and Katrine is such a sweet

girl. We had a picnic lunch, and I've made a list of things she'll need." She paused. "All the same it's a huge place for one girl to be in alone."

Mary's mother was still a little anxious. The whole business was beyond her and it was clear that she thought that Katrine was imagining a great deal, most certainly suspecting their guest without reason.

She was even doubtful of letting her two elder children go back there for the night, though Andrew had to be relieved from duty, as Jim put it, and brought back.

Finally, at about seven, poor Mrs. Carew's admonitions ringing in their ears, Jim and Mary started back again together. Jim rowed a little to the east so that, if Canning were watching, he would not see them until they were too far across to recognise.

Both Katrine and Andrew were in the grounds and rushed up to greet them eagerly.

"It's fun here," Andrew announced. "And Katrine was just going to show me the door to the tower. You *would* come now."

Jim was having no nonsense with his younger brother. He marshalled him down to the boat and homewards.

Katrine took Mary's arm.

"Jim will grow new biceps at this rate. Backwards and forwards across the loch," she remarked, then: "He *is* being decent."

She looked a little pale and tired—perhaps the strain of that first day was telling on her.

There were times when Mary, in the rush of events, forgot the reason for her being there. Now she tried to cheer her up, bringing out the pies her mother had made for their evening meal. They ate in the sitting-room, which they had opened up, and which now looked quite homely in the fading sunlight.

"What was Andrew saying about you showing him

the tower?" asked Mary, after they had finished their meal.

"Well, I had found some great big keys in the kitchen hanging on a nail, and I thought I'd try them."

"You know you mustn't—just mustn't go in the tower," stammered Mary.

Suddenly and frighteningly she was remembering MacShane and his warning. She had promised, and dared not tell Katrine, but for a moment he was very much with her.

"Why all the fuss? When Jim comes back we'll just toddle along and see if one of them fits."

Katrine was a very determined young woman, and when Jim came running up the big stairs, making a clatter as loud as an army, she broached the subject again.

"Let's try one," she pleaded, showing him three very large, very old and very rusty keys.

Jim turned them over.

"You can try, I know they look old, but they're not that old. Why, the tower must date almost to Norman times, at least Norman times in England." He grinned. "The Scots were only savages then, remember."

"Indeed!" Katrine for a moment looked incensed, then her sense of humour got the better of her and she laughed.

But she had won the concession and presently they found their way along the innumerable passages towards the east wing, and then along the narrow, dark, musty-smelling corridor which gave upon the door to the tower.

Katrine took the keys and stepped forward.

It was Mary who noticed that the heavy purple curtain before the door moved a little as in a draught.

Jim pulled the curtain back as Katrine selected a key. Then they all stepped back with a gasp.

The door was not locked, not barred, not even closed —it stood ajar.

Katrine swallowed. "That's funny. It was locked. Who can have opened it?" Head high, she moved forward, but not before Jim had acted.

He caught the door and drew it closed. It banged hollowly.

"Not now, you don't," he said, "we'll wait and explore that place when we've got some other people with us."

"Don't be silly, Jim!"

"I'm not silly, I just don't like it. Anyhow, young woman, you're not going in there to-night!"

"Let's close it, lock it now. In case——" Mary broke off.

"In case what?" asked Katrine, who looked white and frightened.

"In case someone is in there."

It seemed a foolish thing to say but Jim examined the huge ancient lock.

"No key and no bar on this side. We can't." He caught them both by the arm and frog-marched them away.

"Back to headquarters, my hearties, and forget it."

Neither of the girls argued. In fact, when they reached their own little corner in the west wing they were relieved.

Why had the door been left open? Who had been there? Who was it who might still be there? Mary had no answer to these questions.

CHAPTER NINE

THE CASTLE BY NIGHT

It was a great pity, certainly from the girls' point of view, that they had made that strange discovery about the door to the tower.

Luckily Jim was with them and he made light of it.

"After all there's been a gardener in the grounds, and anyone may have come in before we arrived. Anyhow, are you quite sure it was closed the other day?"

"Absolutely," Katrine spoke firmly.

"Oh, well, I suggest we get Mr. Besant or someone to-morrow and we'll all go over the place and exorcise the bogy. Probably the stairs are broken, or the floor's rotten and that's why you've always been warned about the place." He looked at Mary. "What's the matter?"

She could not tell him of the warning she had received. In fact she had not mentioned it to Jim at all, for hadn't she promised? She was silent.

They did not retire until nearly ten, sitting in the pleasant room over the gardens and listening in to Jim's rather battered little portable wireless, talking now and then, although—and it was Jim who steered their conversation into lighter channels—never about their problems.

It was still light when they retired but heavy storm clouds had suddenly risen from the north, and with them came a wind which tossed the trees of the park, and swept across the loch churning it into miniature waves. They could not see the water from that part of the castle but Katrine viewed the coming storm with anxiety.

"The weather's breaking," she said, "it's going to make rowing across difficult."

Jim laughed and flexed his muscles.

"I can take it."

He wished them good night, and before he left them, examined the door of the sitting-room which had a lock and key.

"For your own peace of mind, I should lock it," he advised.

As soon as he had gone Katrine did just that.

"Now we're safe," she laughed uncertainly, "these two rooms are our own little haven."

The bed was big and deep and comfortable. Mary undressed and got in on the side nearest the window, and presently Katrine joined her.

"After all," she murmured sleepily, as the shadows began to descend, "it is rather an adventure."

Mary agreed, also sleepily. It had been a very busy day and she was healthily tired, and, if her last waking thoughts were of the mysteriously open door, they did not keep her awake for long.

Jim had no intention of going to bed yet. Certainly he was tired but far from sleepy. He inspected his room, put out his pyjamas, then sat by the window in the fading light doing an exercise in higher mathematics. He had found, being a clever boy, that using his mind like this passed the time, in the same way as other people did crossword puzzles.

He was waiting for the light to fade. It was past eleven when it was really dark, the darker because of the storm clouds.

Taking his torch, for the electricity was off in the castle, he left his room and went down the corridor and towards the east wing where the tower lay.

He wore gym shoes and made no sound. Reaching the

tower door he cast his torch up and down it. Then he tried it. It was not locked. He hesitated. Should he take this opportunity of exploring the mysterious place?

After a moment, remembering the girls who were, after all, under his protection as he liked to put it, he decided against it. If the place were unsafe and he had an accident it would be very awkward for them. He was no coward but something about the great, old door repelled him. Far better to wait for day and get someone like Ronald Besant to come with them.

Having decided on this, he retraced his steps and found his way down to the kitchen and out by the side door which they used. It was pitch dark in the courtyard but the wind had fallen and now rain was spattering the flags, playing a little tattoo on the leaves of the shrubbery beyond.

He moved round the back and along the gravel path to the front of the big pile.

Moving back from it, he stood some fifty yards away scanning it: it showed a mass just darker than the dark night sky: the graceful Stuart building of the new part, and, to the left, the menacing square of the old tower.

All was silent, nothing moved. Only owls, busy hunting the small night creatures, gave an occasional cry.

He was about to turn away and go in again when he stopped. Almost against his will he had glanced again at the dark shadow of the tower. Surely from one of the slit-like windows so deep in the masonry a light showed?

He waited. Yes, the light was there in the top turret, and, even as he watched, it went out, only to appear in the lower floor. Had the night not been so black he might not have noticed it, for it was a very pale light, probably candlelight or cast by a torch.

So someone was in the tower. But who? Whoever it
was must have been there for some time, but why?

Thinking of the girls he began to hurry, and was
crossing the yard, when he smelt something, the scent
of tobacco smoke. He stopped by an out-size water-butt,
only just in time to see a tall figure move round the
stables and towards the park beyond: just a figure, that
of a tall man who had paused to light his pipe as he stood
in the courtyard, revealing as he did so, a thin
watchful face. Who? One of the tenants, one of the
employees? Unless he were a gamekeeper, it was too
late for the most conscientious worker to be abroad.
Remembering the light in the tower Jim let himself
into the kitchen, closing and locking the door behind
him. It was such an immense place, easy for someone
to conceal himself in one of the rooms, but whoever it
was had not been in the main part of the building but
in the tower.

Jim moved cautiously up and down those innumerable
passages in the direction of the tower wing.

He kept his torchlight down, moving slowly and
quietly, and when he reached the musty-smelling corridor
leading to the tower he switched it out.

Backing into an embrasure by one of the deep-set
windows, he waited. He felt damp, his sweater was
misted with the rain, and, as he waited, he had a terrible
desire to sneeze, and used the old trick of pinching his
nostrils to prevent the threatening explosion. He was
doing this when he heard a creak. The tower door was
being opened.

He tensed, even his desire to sneeze quenched, as he
heard soft padding steps nearing him.

Whoever was coming was using a torch, casting the
light of it straight in front of him.

Jim pressed himself well back. The unknown man did

not suspect his presence, so he was not likely to see him with the beam of the torch in front, casting its circle on the worn carpet, never on the walls.

Nearer and nearer came the figure, then he had passed. Jim had the impression of broad shoulders, of a thick-set figure and a large balding head, thrust forward. That was all he could make out, for the light was in front. But he did know that the man who had passed him on the way from the tower was a stranger to him. He had certainly never seen him before in his life.

He waited, listening. The padding steps went on: he was making for the main staircase.

Silently Jim followed until he reached the gallery, feeling his way as best he could, for he dared not use his torch. The stranger descended the stairs, crossed the hall, played his light on the lock, opened it, and closed it with a quiet thud.

He had gone.

Jim waited. He could do nothing. No use to try and follow him outside, he would soon be lost in the thickly-wooded grounds.

Suddenly he felt very tired. He turned, crossed the gallery and was finding his way to the west wing and bed, when a sound broke the oppressive silence of the great place, a familiar enough sound, sane and ordinary.

Down in the hall the telephone was ringing. Jim turned and rushed back, it was still ringing when he reached the top of the stairs, and it continued to ring as he bounded down, only to stop as he raced to the instrument on the table. Absurdly he remembered Mary's annoyance when just the same thing had happened at the Manse the other day.

He waited a little but it did not ring again, then he slowly went up to bed.

Before going to his room he tried the door of the

sitting-room which led to the girls' bedroom. They had locked it. Good, at least they were safe until morning.

He threw off his damp clothes and all but tumbled into bed.

He slept so heavily that he only awoke when Mary came in. She looked bright and refreshed and was fully dressed, and held a glass of orange juice in her hand.

"Here you are, and Katrine's in the kitchen. She's found an old oil-stove and some paraffin, so we're having tea and a hot meal," she said cheerfully.

Jim stared at her as though he had never seen her before. "Hallo!" He took the drink and downed it thirstily.

"Gosh you do look bleary-eyed," said Mary.

"I know, I slept like the dead."

"It's nearly seven, time you got up. I'm staying with Katrine until nine, then you can come back."

"Come back?"

"Yes. Remember we don't want her left here alone."

"We don't and how!"

Jim spoke so violently that his sister stared.

"Has something happened, Jim?"

"Enough to make me think that Katrine shouldn't be here at all."

She sat on the bed. "Shoot!"

Briefly he told her of his night's experiences: of the light in the tower, of the tall man smoking in the court-yard, and the figure who had left the tower; finally he mentioned the telephone call.

Mary listened, her round face, if possible, lengthening. "Oh, Jim, we ought to make her leave. It's dreadful."

"Are you going to tell her?"

She considered. "Yes," she said at last, "I'm sure she'll see reason and leave if we do. It's all too queer. Perhaps she could go to Mr. Besant." She stopped, thinking of

MacShane. "Jim, that man you saw in the yard? What was he like?"

"Tall, thinnish, tweedy, a moustache, yes I'm sure he had a lightish moustache. He was lighting his pipe and I glimpsed his face."

She nodded. "I've seen him twice, and spoken to him. He's a friend."

"What do you mean? How do you know anyway?"

She hesitated, "I promised."

"Promised? Can't you tell me? After all this has happened?"

"I wish I could see him again"—she paused—"I don't see why I shouldn't tell you. Jim, he's a detective. He asked me a lot of questions, and he was very definite about Katrine keeping away from the castle and especially the tower."

Jim brightened. "So they're still investigating. That's something at any rate. If only we could get in touch with him. Perhaps it was he who rang up last night."

"Perhaps, but where from?"

"The lodge would be the nearest place with a phone," he was saying when Katrine, tall and slim in slacks and a vivid pullover, came in.

"Hallo, you two conspirators," was her greeting.

"Conspirators nothing!" said Jim cheerfully. "What's this about food?"

He did not look at his sister. It was no use startling Katrine now.

"Come and see."

In the sitting-room a small oil-stove glowed on the hearth, surmounted by a large kettle which was already humming.

"I found it in the linen cupboard," she explained, "we'll be able to have tea and I'm boiling some of those super eggs your mother sent. Can you manage two, Jim?"

"I can."

Katrine seemed in better spirits this morning, and they ate a picnic breakfast with good appetite.

Afterwards Jim said, "I'm going to ring the house and get Andrew to send Murdo over."

"But why? Won't you row Mary over and then send him? I shall be all right."

"No." Jim spoke abruptly. "You can't be left alone in this place for one moment. Understand?"

Katrine laughed. "Listen to him! Really, Jim, what could happen to me here?"

"I don't know but there was someone in the tower last night."

Katrine went tense and did not speak. Jim told her his experiences in the night, but Mary noticed that he did not mention his glimpse of the watcher by the court-yard.

"And you saw this man?"

"Yes. A complete stranger, at least to me."

"What was he like?"

"I didn't see him clearly—after all he cast his torchlight ahead of him—but he walked, head forward, though that may have been because of the dark, and he was thick-set and bald. I'm sure he was very bald."

"No one I know either."

Katrine sat very still.

"Katrine, can't you go over to Mr. Besant?" implored Mary. "I'm sure that is the safest thing to do."

"I'll see." Katrine was obstinate. "First of all we've got to explore that tower—we *must*."

Jim stood up. "Not alone. I'll get in touch with Besant and ask him. In fact I think it would be a good idea to tell him everything. Probably he would arrange to have a look in the place. Got his telephone number, Katrine?"

"Glenavar 51. Where are you going?"

He grinned over his shoulder. "To the tower, but not to explore it. I'm getting a thing about that place. Just to see if the door's been left open again."

Once alone, the two girls tidied up mechanically, taking the dirty cups and saucers to the bathroom near.

"You can't go on staying here," said Mary, "it's too uncanny, the whole thing."

"I'll stay to-day, just to-day, then I promise I'll go over to Ronald's."

That at least was something.

"Well, Jim will be with you, and I'll relieve him later on," Mary promised. "You'll have to be careful though, that man Canning is far too interested in this place. He may come over."

"How?"

"He can always hire Murdo."

When Jim strolled back with the news that the door was closed but not locked, they received it with little comment.

"Why was it locked before, and now left open?" was all Katrine said.

Jim did not answer, but Mary at least had had a rather frightening thought, which she was almost certain had occurred to her brother, too. Had it been left open as a trap so that Katrine would explore and find . . . what?

She did not voice this though; instead they all went out into the main part of the castle and Mary rang up the Manse.

Her mother answered her.

"Are you all right, dear?"

"We're fine. But Jim is staying, and could you get Andrew to run down to Murdo and ask him to take over a boat to pick me up? I feel awful at not being with you to help."

"That's all right, dear, we're coping. Two more guests of course to-day."

Mary remembered that the colonel and his wife were coming.

"I'll come as soon as I can to give a hand. How is Mr. Canning?"

"He seems quite content. He intends to go fishing to-day, I believe. But the weather isn't so good, the loch looks quite rough."

There had been so much to discuss that none of them had realised that the sky was grey and a high wind blowing.

"It's just as well then that Murdo will be coming for me," was all Mary said.

Half an hour later all three of them went down to the landing stage. To-day the loch showed a very different aspect, little waves scurried across it like a minature sea, and when Murdo appeared, sculling slowly towards them, he drew up and steadied the boat with a brawny arm, grinning.

"Good day to ye," was his greeting, as he glanced at the boat Jim had come in yesterday. "Ye did weel to call me. 'Tis a harrd pull across the day!"

Mary jumped in, "Will it get any better?"

"Aye, but there's nae tellin'." He waved and cast off.

Mary herself waved until the figures of Jim and Katrine were hidden by the trees. They curved round, and moved across the rough waters. She rather enjoyed the rocking of the boat, reflecting that she was, luckily, a good sailor, and when the Manse came into view she had again a little happy feeling to think that this now was home. Even on that grey day it looked welcoming, and Andrew was on the lawn in front playing with his kitten.

He raced up.

"How's everything? When can I go over?" he asked.

"I expect Jim will give us a ring, then you can come over with me."

"What happened?" he asked, noticing perhaps something about her expression which puzzled him.

"Nothing, nothing at all. But you know that Katrine can't be left."

Andrew caught up his cat.

"The Canning character's acting oddly," he announced.

"In what way?"

He indicated the road which ran by their house towards the village. "Ever since breakfast he's been strolling up and down, smoking cigarettes. Mary, it looks to me as though he's on the lookout for someone."

Mary nodded. "Andrew, you can help. Can you keep an eye on him, and see if he does meet anyone? You can keep well out of sight if you try."

"I know just the place, a copse of trees on that hillock, bracken all round them. Shall I go now?"

"Yes, do, Andrew. It really is important."

He put Boodle in her arms. "Keep an eye on her for me," he said, then he slipped away and was soon hidden in the trees.

As soon as she got inside the Manse, Mother was there, full of questions.

Mary told her as much as she dared. That the tower room was open, that they suspected that it was dangerous, perhaps with rotten steps or floors, and that Katrine had to be watched in case she ventured in it.

Mother was very uneasy.

"It's all very worrying. She mustn't stay there another day. If she still feels that she cannot come back here, and I'm sure I don't know why, for Mr. Canning seems most innocuous, she had better go back to her aunt."

"Yes, Mummy," Mary spoke soothingly," as a matter of fact she promised that she won't stay for more than a day now."

There was plenty to do in the Manse. The large room allotted to the new guests expected that day had been prepared, and Mary got busy helping with the washing-up, laying the table ready for lunch, and making herself useful in every way she could.

She was busy cleaning up one of the bathrooms when Andrew came to find her. Andrew was bursting with news.

"He's talking to a car," he said absurdly.

"What do you mean?"

"Come quickly! It stopped beyond the bend and he went up to it and began to talk to the people in it. Two people."

"What were they like?"

"A man and a woman. The woman's got yellow hair, but oldish, I'd say. So's the man, he's bald, never seen him before."

A bald man! Mary remembered Jim's description of the intruder last night.

She threw down the cloth and the scouring powder, and hurried out. Together she and Andrew raced out of the house then took to the bank of trees which followed the road.

Andrew moved ahead, keeping well-hidden from the road, then, going down in a crouching position, he waved Mary down, too.

"You can see through these bushes. They're still there. The driver's got out."

Mary stared down at the road. A long low car, an old Daimler, stood there, and, strolling by it, up and down, up and down, was Mr. Canning, cigarette in mouth. With him was a short thick-set man who walked, head forward, hands clasped behind him, a man with a large, almost completely bald, head.

They were talking, those two, very seriously, but neither Mary nor Andrew could hear what they were saying.

Then, as they watched, the bald man turned and got back into the car, started it and slowly drove on and past the Manse. Canning crushed out his cigarette and followed it.

"What do you make of it?" asked Andrew.

"I don't know. I wish Jim were here," Mary spoke half to herself, staring across the still-rough loch to the distant tower of the castle.

Had that man in the car been the one whom Jim had seen in the castle last night? She had no idea, but if he were, it meant, she felt instinctively, danger for Katrine.

CHAPTER TEN

THE ROOM OF THE MIRROR

MARY RETURNED to the house and went straight to the telephone only to find that Lilian was using it, giving an order to the village store.

"And who do you want to ring, dear?" she asked, when she had finished her call.

"I want to get Jim at the castle."

Lilian's pleasant face clouded. "Really this is all very worrying. I'm sure it isn't good for that poor child to be alone there."

"She's promised to make other arrangements after to-day."

"I should think so. At present you children are as elusive as minnows, and poor Helen is very anxious." She brightened. "Anyhow the new guests will soon be here. I do hope they are satisfied."

"Sure to be, Aunt Lilian."

With all her thoughts centred on the various odd happenings, Mary had all but forgotten, if only for the time, that this lovely new home of theirs was a business proposition which must succeed.

All the same she rang the castle, heard the phone ring and ring to no answer, then put it down again. Probably Jim and Katrine were in the grounds. But she would have given much to tell Jim of what she had seen.

Mr. Canning strolled in as she turned away, and offered her a pleasant good morning, his white smile in his red face reminding her more than ever of that of an over-wily fox.

As Colonel and Mrs. Brayne arrived in their own car by ten-thirty that morning she had no time to try and phone again. They proved to be quite satisfied with their room and the small sitting-room set aside for them.

The colonel was a rather slight man with a shrewd thin face, and his wife was white-haired, charming and friendly. Watching her mother and Lilian talking to them, Mary could see that these guests, at least, would give no trouble. The colonel, it seemed, had been seriously ill and needed a quiet place in which to convalesce.

She left her mother and his wife discussing his necessary diet and went into the kitchen to see if she could help with the lunch. Lilian was there, prodding a veal stew.

"So fortunate I ordered veal, with the colonel so delicate," she remarked. "Yes, dear, you can do the vegetables, wash the greens, please. Andrew has been angelic and done the potatoes."

Mary did the greens, whipped up some whites of eggs for a souffle, then as it was nearly twelve, decided to make her call again. Surely Katrine and Jim would be in the castle by now; the day was still grey and not really warm enough for wandering about the grounds.

The hall was empty and the door closed. Mary made her call again and this time, after half a minute interval, Katrine answered.

"Hallo, darling, could you send over a pie or something? Jim's hungry—we've been exploring the park—and I don't want to give him eggs again."

"If you can wait, I'll get over by two, and bring something. Everything O.K., Katrine?"

"Yes and no. Jim's tried to get Ronald but he isn't in. Any news on your side?"

"Yes, that Canning man, if that's his name, has been talking to some strangers. I rather want to tell Jim about them."

"He's not very far away. Hold on and I'll get him."

"Well, how's tricks?" Jim sounded cheerful enough, but when Mary told him of the bald, thick-set man who had been, as she put it, "in cahoots" with the man Katrine was so sure had followed her all the way from London, he took it very seriously.

"The trouble is," he said, "that I'd have to see him to be sure, but I do think, if it was the man I saw here last night, I'd know."

"As far as I know they've driven on and away," replied Mary.

"Look here, I couldn't contact Besant, but he should be in for lunch. I'll try again now, then I'll row over."

"But we can't leave Katrine—we really can't!"

"If she locked herself in those rooms . . ." Jim began.

"Just try her, she'd probably start getting curious about the tower again."

"Yes, she just might. Better keep to the old plan then, get Murdo to row you and Andrew over at two then I'll come back with him. Might be as well to keep a boat on this side."

"Have you seen anyone in the grounds?"

"Nary a one! Even the old gardener seems to have downed tools to-day."

Mary put back the receiver and went back to her work. Dinner was served to their three guests. The colonel and his wife, after exchanging a few polite words with Mr. Canning, kept to themselves. By the time they had cleared and sat down to their own lunch it was nearly half past one.

Mary remained to help with the washing-up, then, collecting Andrew, she went along to the boat-house to find Murdo. Luckily he was free, for the weather had not tempted any passing motorists to go on the loch, and he stroked them across. He was obviously curious about their comings and goings.

"The young lass shouldnae linger on her ain there," he remarked portentiously. "All this pother and the polis a-comin' and a-goin'."

"Police?" asked Andrew.

"Aye, have ye no' seen them then? Pokin' and pryin', and still nae news of the Maclure."

"I haven't seen any," Andrew sounded resentful.

Murdo bent over the oars. "'Tis nae wonder what wi' yer fishin' and sich." He looked at Mary. "Heard the news?"

"What news?"

"The inspector man from Perth was shot in yon castle grounds last nicht, I did hear. Could be a poacher, but I'm nae sae sure, it's an unchancy place, ye ken, now the Maclure's nae mair."

"Was his name MacShane?" asked Mary.

"Mebbe, mebbe, I am nae sure." Murdo relapsed into silence, bending his broad shoulders to the oars.

Mary was frightened. Jim had seen MacShane in the castle grounds last night, he had also seen the stranger leaving the tower. The two incidents had a sinister significance.

Andrew was busy asking questions again.

"Murdo, what do *you* think happened to Mr. Maclure?"

The big man shrugged, watching the water drip from his oars. "I dinna ken. 'Twas an evil day when he was speerited awa', goodness knows where."

They were approaching the boat-house where Jim stood waiting. Before getting into the boat he drew Mary aside and, before she could tell him her sinister news, said:

"Any sign of those people again?"

"No, none at all. We shouldn't even have known about

them if Andrew hadn't noticed that Canning seemed to be waiting on the road. But listen, Jim. Remember you saw MacShane, that detective, for I'm sure it was he, last night?"

"Of course."

"Murdo just told me he was shot, here in these grounds last night."

"Good life, killed?"

"No, no I don't think so. Jim, don't tell Katrine!"

"Might be a good idea, she would come away then. She *is* going to ring Besant anyhow." He frowned. "By the way, where is she?"

"Coming down that slope. Jim, what had we better do? Tell the police about what you saw?"

"I suppose I could ring up Perth, no use contacting the village."

"But the police are about, Murdo says so."

"I'll have to think it over, may run into one if I keep my eyes skinned, but they seem pretty elusive. I'll pump Murdo a bit as we go over."

Katrine came up at that moment, so Jim got in the boat and was rowed away.

As the two girls and Andrew strolled to the castle Mary told her of the latest development, though she did not mention MacShane's being shot. She described the man in the car but Katrine had no idea who it could be.

"I know that Canning followed me, though. I suppose he's no idea I'm here?"

"He can't have."

They went up to what Katrine called her suite and unpacked the food Mary had brought. As she ate the cold pie and drank the instant coffee they had brought, Katrine discussed the whole chain of incidents.

"Jim and I have been talking things over," she said, "and try as we can we can't make head nor tail of it all.

Why should these strangers follow me up here? I know that people, my friends, that is, don't want me to be here on my own, that's common sense. But why should these strangers be on my track?"

Mary hesitated. But Andrew spoke for her. "Perhaps you're right and your father was—well it wasn't an accident and they don't want you to find out what happened," he said.

Katrine nodded. "Yes, that's the conclusion I've come to," she said soberly.

"But no one knows what did happen to him."

Katrine stared at her coffee. "And that's what I still mean to find out. Mary, if only I dared!"

"Dared what?"

"Dared go into the tower."

"You mustn't—you know you mustn't!"

"Can't we just take a peep?" said Andrew excitedly.

"No, not even a peep." Mary was very firm. "Jim is right, you know. We ought to have someone with us if we do venture in."

"I suppose so. I'll try and get Ronald. He should be at home this afternoon."

That afternoon the two girls spent in going over the many splendid rooms of the castle.

By this time real friendship had warmed between Katrine and Mary. And as the older girl showed her from one room to another, from the great library where books, many valuable, practically walled the room, to the gallery where those pictures of Katrine's ancestors looked down at the last Maclure, they talked of more than the castle itself.

Katrine was showing Mary the portrait of Beatrice Maclure, a lovely woman who had lived in the time of Queen Victoria.

"Strange," she said, "she wanted to be a doctor, but of

course in those days no one had heard of women doctors. Instead she married my great-great-great-grandfather and had seven children. Two of the boys were killed in the Indian Mutiny, two died when they were children, but she still managed to help in the village. She was a wonderful nurse and had a real knowledge of medicine."

"What would you like to be?" asked Mary.

"Oh that's what I meant, I want to be a doctor. But I don't know now."

"Surely there's nothing to prevent you?"

"No, perhaps not. The estate isn't even settled yet, and I'm a minor. Father said I could follow my bent. I think he rather liked the idea."

She fell silent as she always did when she mentioned her father.

"Jim wants to be a doctor," said Mary. "Perhaps if the Manse is successful he will be."

"Why not? He could go to Edinburgh to study."

"Yes, but he was talking of giving up the idea."

"Why, for goodness' sake?"

"Money, just money. He was thinking of getting work as soon as he leaves school."

"He mustn't," Katrine spoke almost sharply, "I've got lots of money, at least I think so. There's property in Edinburgh as well as all this. I can help."

Mary laughed. "You're sweet, but he wouldn't like that."

"What's the good of money if one can't help with it?"

They strolled on along the gallery and, coming out at the head of the stairs, Katrine went to one of the long windows with the upper part showing their armorial bearings in bright stained glass and looked down at the end of the terrace below.

"I thought I heard a car," she said.

She had scarcely spoken when the heavy jangling bell from the front door was rung.

As they hurried down the stairs, Katrine said, "By the way, where's Andrew? He was with us before we entered the gallery."

Mary stared back. No sign of Andrew.

But the bell rang again and Katrine crossed the wide hall and began to struggle with bolts and lock. They always used the back door, and this one being big and heavy took some force to open.

At last she flung it wide and there, looking rather grim, his car in the drive behind him, stood Ronald Besant.

"Hallo, what are you doing here, Katrine?"

Katrine was at once on the defensive:

"How did you know I was here? As a matter of fact we did try to get you on the phone."

"You did?" he sounded unbelieving. "Are you actually staying here?"

"Yes, but not alone. The Carews are taking turns to be with me. Come up to my quarters. I've been using the oriel suite."

Smiling at Mary he followed them in silence and, once in the sitting-room which Katrine had made comfortable in spite of the incongruous oil-heater on the hearth, he said abruptly:

"Now, what is all this? You know I warned you not to come here."

"Don't be absurd, Ronald, I'm safer here than anywhere else."

"Seen any police this morning?"

"Police? No. Why?"

"Their principal C.I.D. man was shot not far from the lodge last night."

"Killed?"

"No, he was wounded above the heart luckily, but it doesn't recommend this place as a refuge. As you know, the villagers may take a salmon or two but we've no poachers to speak of."

Katrine stared at him, then she said, "It's dreadful. Was it someone investigating Daddy's . . ." she stopped.

"Yes, I told you the police have not given up. And you, my dear, are only an embarrassment to them. Now be a good girl and go back to the Manse, you'll be all right there."

Mary watched them. Mr. Besant looked both angry and troubled.

"I can't," Katrine said in low tones, "I've been followed here. Yes, someone was watching me at the school and he followed me on the train. I gave him the slip, but now he's here, staying at the Manse as a guest."

"My dear girl, this sounds extraordinary. What is he like anyway?"

Katrine described him succinctly.

"Red face, thin features, dark receding hair."

He shook his head. "A complete stranger obviously. There is such a thing as coincidence. He was travelling to Perth, and he came on to the Manse. Aren't you being a little over-suspicious?"

"No, I'm not. I know it's the same man I saw in the school grounds. He is, isn't he, Mary?"

"I'm almost certain he is," Mary agreed.

Ronald Besant sat down and took out a cigarette.

"Now let's get this straight. You think you have been followed here by this unknown character. Why, Katrine, why?"

"I don't know, only I feel it has something to do with Father going like this."

"And there was someone in the tower last night," added Mary.

Ronald's grey eyes darkened. "Sure? Best thing is for me to contact the police—if only MacShane had not been shot . . ." he broke off. "Look here, Katrine, you'd better come to my place where I can keep an eye on you. Biddy will see to you, remember Biddy?"

"Of course." Katrine paused. "Ronald, if I do, will you help me?"

"How?"

"To find out about Father . . ."

He got up and strolled to the window, turned and was about to answer her when, faintly from below through the open door came the sound of faint ringing. It was the telephone.

Ronald Besant turned quickly, "I'll get it," he said, hurrying out and down the corridor.

Luckily this time the caller was persistent and it was still ringing as he reached the hall.

The girls, coming down after him, found him talking into it urgently.

"Asking for me? Are you sure? Not sure? Biddy, what do you mean? Better get Dr. Forsyth at once. Do your best for him . . . I'll be over within twenty minutes."

He put back the receiver.

There was a very strange expression on his face: he looked both perplexed and excited if that were possible. Katrine must have sensed something unusual too, for she asked:

"What is the matter?"

"I don't know yet. Someone to see me. I must go."

He glanced at them both, "Katrine, go back to the Manse before night. Will you promise?"

"I can't unless that man isn't there. It will be all right really, Mary and Jim will be with me."

"Jim is coming over later," Mary told him. "Don't worry, please, we won't let her out of our sight."

His mind seemed to be on some new problem of his own, he only nodded almost vaguely.

"See you later," was all he said, as he crossed the hall and went out. They heard him start his car and drive off.

Katrine linked her arm in Mary's.

"What do you make of that?"

"I don't know. That telephone call upset him."

Katrine said nothing more. Had the call anything to do with their quest? That was the thought in both their minds as they returned to Katrine's quarters. They had reached the landing when Mary stopped.

"Katrine, where is Andrew?"

Suddenly they both realised that they had not seen him for more than an hour. He had been with them when they first came, even sat eating biscuits when Katrine took her long-delayed lunch; and for a time he had wandered about inspecting the beautiful, formal rooms, then suddenly he had just vanished.

"Perhaps he's in the grounds," offered Katrine.

Mary had had a frightening thought, "The tower—he's terribly interested in it—suppose he's gone to the tower!"

"We'll look!" Katrine led the way across the castle, up and down stairs, and along innumerable passages until they reached the rather grim and gloomy corridor to the tower. The heavy curtains were pulled aside and the door was ajar. Both girls hesitated.

Mary ventured in and, finding herself facing worn stone steps which wound upwards, paused and called, "Andrew!"

"The walls are very thick," said Katrine, who had followed her, "let's go up."

The steps spiralled up, lit here and there by slits in the masonry, then suddenly they saw daylight, and a final turn brought them on to a square platform. In the centre was an iron flagstaff and all around the tessellated walls of the tower.

The view was very fine: they could see the distant village with the small crofts round it, and the road winding past the Manse. They could see the Manse itself, its peaked roofs wet in the dull light and to their left, the loch, gloomy to-day and churning to the very foot of three sides of the tower.

Mary turned away—the vista was fascinating, but there was no sign of Andrew.

Katrine was already moving down the stairs again.

"He may be below," she said over her shoulder.

Reaching the bottom of the steps near the door through which they had come, Katrine indicated the stairs winding down: they looked dark and sinister.

They circled for about forty feet then abruptly found themselves in a square room.

The walls were hung with crumbling tapestry, and the light came from narrow slit-like and glassless windows twenty feet up. In one corner was an ancient wooden chair winged and carved, in another a deep chest. Immediately opposite them was a door, an arched doorway in the masonry, which moved a little from some unsuspected draught.

Katrine stared at it, fascinated, and was moving towards it when it opened wide, and she stepped back, her hand to her mouth to muffle a scream.

"Hallo?" What are you doing here?"

It was Andrew.

Mary caught his arm, relieved and angry, too.

"What on earth do you mean by going off like that?"

He was excited. "I've been exploring. Come and see."

"What is down there?"

He shuffled a little and Mary saw that he was nervous and trying to hide it.

"It's kind of funny," he said, "but quite safe, really."

"Come on," cried Katrine, "if Andrew can go down there so can we." She was already moving towards the door.

They followed her down more steps, circling into darkness faintly lit by the narrow lancet holes; this time the stairs wound thrice between walls which glistened wetly and in air which smelt humid and unwholesome.

"What's that?" asked Mary, as they completed the second turn.

There was a low hissing noise.

"It's the loch water," Andrew told them, "this part is built right out of the loch."

The third bend led straight into another room, if such it could be called; certainly it had four walls, but it was dimmer, though lancets, as in the room above, gave a diffused light.

The stone floor was seeping with water, lichen grew in the crevices and it was completely empty save for four ancient iron rings in one wall. From one dangled a heavy chain broken and eaten with rust.

"Look at that door!" cried Andrew. There was yet another door. It was narrow, arched and firmly set in the thick walls, but something about it was different—it was like no door, ancient or modern that they had ever seen.

In the upper part was a circle, stained and green with the damp.

Katrine stared at it, then bent near to examine it. "Look," she said, "it's of some kind of metal."

She took her handkerchief, moistened it, and rubbed.

It was bronze, and the white of her handkerchief and even her finger was reflected dully in it.

"Why, it's a kind of mirror!" exclaimed Mary.

Katrine recoiled.   Even in the faint light she looked pale.

Andrew broke in cheerfully—his spirits had risen in their company.

"There are words kind of written round it but I can't quite make them out."

Katrine had moved away silently.

Mary peered; then, using her own handkerchief, cleaned round the oval.   Andrew was right: words had been etched by some sharp instrument round the edge of the bronze mirror which took up half the surface of the door.

At last she was able to read them.

"How very strange," she said.   "Listen, this is what it says."

Slowly she read the words:

> "*If loch be high,*
> *There's greetin' nigh,*
> *Tak nae step doon*
> *Frae nicht tae noon.*"

"Yes, I think that's what it says.   Katrine, what does it mean?"

Katrine turned on them.

"Let's go," she said.   "Don't you understand?   It's the Room of the Mirror!"

"Can't we go through the door?" asked Andrew.

"No!"   Katrine laughed, but the sound was high and a little hysterical.   "No, I don't think we will.   Come on, let's leave this awful place."   She stopped as she went across to the steps which would lead them up and out again, and bent down.

She stood for what seemed a long time staring at what she had picked up.

She was so quiet that Mary went up to her.

"What is it, Katrine?" she queried in a worried tone.

Silently Katrine opened her hand; in it lay a small round medallion, a gold medallion, with a small bit of broken chain.

"It looks very old—a Greek coin maybe, or is it Roman?"

"It belonged to my father. He found it when he was fighting in Sicily during the landings there. He said it was his luck." Katrine spoke mechanically.

"But what is it doing here?"

"He carried it on his key chain."

She turned and walked slowly up the stairs. Brother and sister followed.

"I say," said Andrew, "she does seem upset. What does it mean?"

Mary stared at Katrine's dark head as she moved ahead. She thought she knew what it meant. Katrine had found a clue at last to her father's disappearance. She had found it in the ill-famed Room of the Mirror. No wonder she was shaken.

CHAPTER ELEVEN

VISITORS FOR KATRINE

It was good to be in the main part of the castle again. It was Mary who closed that sinister door, drew the curtains across it, and with Andrew, followed Katrine, who as though walking in a dream, went towards the rooms they had made their own.

Mary was puzzled. Certainly she understood Katrine's reaction when she had found the medallion, but before that, when they had discovered the bronze mirror in the door to the lowest room in the tower, she had been very strange.

When they reached the sitting-room, they found that the sun had come out, but the wind still blew, and heavy clouds promised more rain.

The pleasant sitting-room with its comfortable chairs, the odds and ends of groceries and food piled in a corner, made a great contrast to that ancient tower with its thick walls dripping with moisture, its dimness, its very eerieness.

Looking at Katrine's pale face Mary said cheerfully, "Let's make some tea."

She went and filled the kettle from the bathroom and, lighting the oil-stove, put it on.

"It was a funny place," remarked Andrew, "gave me the jitters. It was fun on the top, I spent quite a time up there identifying places around, but when I went right down! Golly, I was jolly glad when I heard you girls."

Katrine did not speak. She sat turning the medallion she had found over and over in her hand.

"Anyhow," went on Andrew, "if that is the Room of

the Mirror, I don't think much of it. Just a piece of bronze."

"In the olden days they used bronze for mirrors," his sister told him. "I expect it was put there before glass was invented."

"That's a thought. When was it invented?"

Trust Andrew to ask awkward questions! Mary was thinking this out when Katrine spoke at last.

"I'm not quite sure. But when Mary Queen of Scots came to Holyrood House, she missed the glass windows in France, I seem to remember that."

"Anyhow," said Mary, "I'm glad you didn't venture there alone."

"My father must have gone there alone," said Katrine.

"Well, he might have at any time. I mean it couldn't have much to do with his disappearance." Mary tried to sound matter-of-fact.

"That medallion . . . he used to laugh and say it brought him luck. It was on the shores of Sicily and when he saw it in the sand, he bent to pick it up, and missed a sniper who would have killed him."

Mary was buttering some bread.

"At least you'll have something to tell Mr. Besant, perhaps he'll go down the tower now," she said.

"Perhaps, but remember what he said? I think he does know what happened to Father."

Mary went to her side and gently took the medallion from her.

"Katrine please, don't grieve so! You must get out of this place, it's so big, and being alone here is enough to make you miserable."

Katrine smiled. "You're a dear, Mary. I wish I could go back with you to the Manse."

"So do I. Never mind, you'll be going to Mr. Besant's soon. Who is Biddy, by the way?"

"His housekeeper. She used to be a maid here, but now she and her husband manage for Ronald. She's rather a pet."

They were still having their tea when a clatter on the stairs heralded the appearance of Jim.

He stood in the doorway and grinned at them all. "All hail, my hearties," he said. "How's everything? I bear news."

"I hope it's good," said Mary.

Katrine looked at him unsmiling.

"What's up, everybody? Is this a wake or something?" he asked.

"We've been in the tower," explained Mary, "and Katrine found something of her father's there. It gave her a shock."

He was immediately serious. "She did? What was it, Katrine?"

Silently she handed him the medallion. "It has been broken off his key-ring," she said. "It's a clue. He *was* in the tower, and he never went in it. Hated the place."

"And there's another door to another room right down, and a mirror on it in bronze," added Andrew. "Jim, when was glass invented?"

"Interesting," Jim, having examined the golden disc, gave it back to Katrine. "If the police went down there they must have overlooked it. I suggest we discuss everything when we get back to the Manse. Hear that, Katrine?"

"Yes. What do you mean?"

"I told you I had good news. Our friend Canning has left. Yes, at three o'clock precisely this afternoon. Packed bag and baggage and vamoosed. Said that urgent business re-called him to London. Not that he had had any letters or phone calls as far as we know."

Katrine brightened immediately when she heard this. "Are you sure?"

"Certain sure. Away he went—our first guest and he couldn't stand it any longer."

"Nonsense!" Mary spoke lightly, for this was very good news. "I expect he had other fish to fry. Anyhow you can come back with us, Katrine, think of that!"

"It's wonderful, but I'll have to let Ronald know. As a matter of fact I didn't relish another night here."

Jim helped himself to a cup of tea.

"Had to get Murdo again, but the boat is waiting. It's still a bit choppy, but I'll row you over whenever you so desire, Miss Maclure." He bowed absurdly and Katrine smiled for the first time since her discovery in the tower.

It was nearly five and there was nothing to keep them in the castle, so Mary got busy tidying up the rooms which had been their refuge and certainly Katrine's, for the last two days, whilst Katrine herself packed her bag.

The sun was shining as they crossed the park towards the landing-stage, and got into the waiting boat. It was quite deserted with no sign of any police, although one of their men had been injured there last night. Thinking of MacShane, Mary felt sorry and hoped he was recovering all right, Ronald Besant had seemed to think so anyway.

Meanwhile Jim sculled them across and when they saw the roofs of the Manse across the water Mary could have cheered.

Although she had been away for a few hours only, so much seemed to have happened that it might have been days.

Both Mother and Lilian greeted them, especially Katrine, with relief.

"Certainly our first guest didn't stay long," Mother said wryly, "but I can't help feeling glad you're with us again, my dear. I never did like you being all alone in that great place."

"But I wasn't alone," Katrine reminded her. "Everyone rallied round marvellously."

So Katrine was installed again in her own room, and Mary hurried off to see if she could help in the kitchen.

Colonel and Mrs. Brayne had gone out in the afternoon in their car, but would be back for dinner which had to be prepared.

Mary was in fact helping Lilian with the meal when Jim came in.

"I'd like a word with you when you're finished," he said.

So when she had finished, after a final glance at the guests' table in the dining-room, she strolled out into the garden with Jim.

"Katrine's in her room," he remarked. "I wanted a consultation with you alone about all this."

"What do you make of it?" asked Mary.

"I'd like a description, in words of one syllable, of that tower place first," he told her.

She described their discoveries as best she could, even trying to remember the odd little verse round the bronze mirror of the door.

"We'll have to explore the lowest chamber, that's certain," he said. "I wonder if the police went down there?"

Mary's hand flew to her throat.

"Jim, you don't mean that he, Katrine's father, might still be down there?"

"I don't know. Let's face it, it is a possibility. But don't look so frightened, I'm almost certain the police would search there."

"But Katrine says he never went there—it was always shut. Perhaps she's thought of that, too."

"Perhaps, poor kid! Now don't let's look on the blackest side. The whole set-up is a mystery: that man following her, his meeting those people, the light in the tower I saw. And MacShane being shot. I wonder how he is getting on?"

"Ronald Besant was going to see him, I know."

"Yes, by the way, Katrine rang him to say she was back here."

"Was he pleased?"

"She didn't say."

They strolled up and down, deep in discussion, though not coming to any satisfactory conclusions. When Katrine, seeing them from her window, came down to join them, Jim began to talk lightly of this and that, careful not to touch on the subject uppermost in all their minds.

The Braynes returned, dined and retired early. Katrine had her meal with the family in their own room.

After clearing up and leaving the kitchen tidy and clean for the morrow, Mary felt ready for bed although it was still light.

Andrew seemed to have forgotten his experience in the tower when he discovered that Boodle had done her good deed for the day and caught a mouse which she had, untactfully, brought in and tried to put on Lilian's knee during dinner.

Finally they all went to bed early. Certainly, for the younger members of the household, it had been an eventful day, and Mary at least was glad it was over.

The next day was to be, in its way, just as eventful; perhaps it was fortunate that none of them could foresee this.

Katrine and the family had breakfast at eight; the

guests, after being served morning tea, had theirs at nine.

Mary had plenty to do, as had Jim, who helped to carry water up to the various bedrooms, and stoke the stove.

It was a beautiful day again, the sun shone, though the loch was still choppy, and, so clear was it, that the purple-tipped hills seemed to be deceptively near and the lovely mountain Benavar rose beyond, its summit unclouded by mist.

Katrine, after trying without success to give a hand, had wandered into the garden, and when Mary called her in for a cup of tea, she turned smiling.

"The old mountain is clear to-day—usually it means rain," she said.

She had not discussed her problem this morning, there had been no time. Even when they had lunch the talk was general, Mother and Lilian discussing further applications they had for guests.

"At this rate we shall have a full house by the end of August," said Lilian with satisfaction.

"If they are all as nice as the Braynes you have nothing to worry about," Katrine remarked.

She had been talking to them that morning. She did not mention that they had been curious about the castle: everyone who came to the district was curious about her home, if it came to that.

That afternoon, with Mother and her friend resting in their sitting-room, Jim wandered about restlessly, then came up to Katrine and Mary who were sitting in the garden.

"Katrine," he said without preamble. "What about me going over to Ronald Besant? I'd like to talk over things with him."

Katrine frowned. "What things? When I rang him

last night he was definitely cagey. I--I think something has happened."

"What do you mean ... something?" asked Jim quickly. "I don't know. He had a call at the castle and he was odd after that."

"Nonsense. Did you tell him about the tower and what you found there?"

"No. It's always difficult on the phone. And Jeannie, on the exchange in the village, listens to everything."

"Well, all the better to go and see him. Why not come with me?"

Katrine was singularly unenthusiastic.

"I don't think I will. You can if you like."

"Why don't you want to go?" asked Mary.

"I don't know." Her dark eyes clouded: she was afraid that Ronald had found out something new, afraid perhaps of the truth.

Meanwhile Jim stood waiting urgently.

"All right," she said at last, "you go. Give him my love and tell him, if you like, what I found in the tower. Perhaps it doesn't matter now."

Andrew, cat circling round him, came in at that moment.

"Go where?" he asked.

"To Glenavar to see Mr. Besant. Like to come, too? We'll cycle."

"Fine. How do we get there?"

Katrine got up and indicated the road which wound past the loch.

"It's in the opposite direction to the village. Go past Murdo's boat-house, continue straight on, then turn at the crossroads to the north. It's about eight miles."

"Good." Jim turned to leave.

"Tell him I'm all right here and that I don't intend to leave," said Katrine.

"O.K.", said Jim as he sprang on to his bicycle.

They watched the boys cycle up the drive, then Mary said, "I thought you liked Mr. Besant?"

"I do. But, like everyone else, he doesn't want me here. He doesn't understand that I must know what has happened."

"He should. I would in your place," Mary paused, "Katrine, don't look like that!"

Katrine lay back, eyes closed and rather pale. "I'm all right. Just tired, I suppose."

Mary felt helpless. There was so little she could do. When her mother and Lilian came into the garden and were joined by the colonel and his wife who had elected to stay in that day, she was pleased to see them.

It was decided that they were to have tea in the garden, and the two girls got busy bringing out more chairs and the small iron table from the shed. Together they made the tea and served it.

Their guests talked pleasantly of their plans. The colonel meant to do some fishing and Mrs. Brayne was enthusiastic about the castle.

"It would be so nice, my dear," she said to Katrine, "if you could take us round."

"I will," Katrine agreed politely, "but the caretakers will be back next week. I must get them to tidy up the place, then you can see it at its best."

"To think that it belongs now to a young girl like you!" went on Mrs. Brayne, her faded blue eyes kindly.

Lilian broke in quickly.

"Katrine is not used to the idea yet. Did you say you wanted me to show you how to make bannocks, Mrs. Brayne?"

She had changed the conversation tactfully and, for

the next few minutes, they talked of cooking and Scottish cooking especially.

It was nearly five, the Braynes had gone inside as the wind had turned a little fresh and the tea things had been cleared into the kitchen, when the car drove up.

Mary was in the kitchen busy washing up. Katrine had gone to her room to change out of her slacks for the evening, when the sound of a car reached her.

Reflecting that it would be Ferguson with a chicken he had promised them for the morrow, Mary went on with her chores.

It was Lilian who brought the news. She entered in some excitement.

"Mary, more guests—unexpected—well, not exactly unexpected. Such a surprise for Katrine!"

Lilian could be vague, though she was practical enough in everyday affairs.

"What do you mean, Aunt Lilian?"

"Didn't you hear the car?"

"I did hear a car, but I thought it was Ferguson."

"It's a Mr. Maclure and his wife. Surely you remember Katrine's aunt in London ringing her to tell her they were coming? Well, they're here, talking to her now."

"The cousins from New Zealand?"

"Yes."

Mary pulled off her apron. "What are they like?"

"I only glimpsed them. He's about forty, but bald which makes him look older, she's fair and rather pretty. They're making quite a fuss of Katrine."

Mary hesitated. She couldn't very well burst into what would, after all, be a family meeting. So she slipped up the back stairs to change, for, like Katrine, she had worn slacks all day. It was when she looked out of the window and saw the car that she had her first suspicion.

It stood in the drive, a large Daimler. Surely it was the same car she and Andrew had seen on the road only the other day, the car which had stopped for the elusive Mr. Canning?

Perhaps it was not the same, she had not noticed the registration number, and it was the kind hired out to tourists, she did know that.

She slipped on a frock, smoothed her fair hair, gave herself a cursory glance in the mirror, then hurried down.

Voices came from the lounge, a man's voice, quite soft and pleasant, and Katrine's.

Her mother came out of the room as Mary reached the foot of the stairs.

"Go and meet Katrine's relatives, dear," she said, "they are staying so I must get their room ready. Such a pleasant surprise for her, it will take her mind off things."

She hurried upstairs and Mary forced herself, for it felt like that, to go into the lounge.

Katrine sat by the window, rather tense, but talking to a broad-set man with a heavy, rather pallid face and a head almost completely bald. The woman, who sat on the window seat next to Katrine, was short, too, and rather stout, with faded fair hair and a once pretty face. She wore a rather fussy summer frock under a duster coat and played nervously with strings of beads round her neck.

Mary aghast, stood in the doorway, for the man was the man she and Andrew had seen talking to Mr. Canning, the man they suspected of being the one Jim had glimpsed coming from the tower. She had no time to speculate about what this might mean, for Katrine called her.

"Mary, do come in. These are my cousins from New Zealand—you remember Aunt Enid rang up about them."

Mary came forward. Mr. Maclure stood up and held out a podgy hand.

"Well, well, how fortunate that dear Katrine has such nice friends. I must say that when I heard that she was at Lendaloch I had some misgivings, but now I understand. I had feared, yes feared, that she was at the castle."

"No, she is staying with us," said Mary unnecessarily.

Katrine broke in. "As a matter of fact I have been staying at the castle for a bit."

The woman spoke for the first time. "Really, but how very brave of you!"

"Why brave?" Katrine raised her dark brows.

Mr. Maclure coughed. "Myra means that it is a huge place and must be lonely, especially now."

Mary sat and listened, studying the newcomers. Was she being too suspicious? For she did not like either of them. The man was ingratiating, the woman merely echoing his words and manner. But Katrine seemed to accept them, and was quite at ease.

At last she got up and excused herself, leaving the man describing their life in New Zealand where he had a sheep station, whilst Katrine listened politely.

Mechanically she went upstairs to help her mother prepare their room. If only the boys would return! If Jim recognised the man as the one who had been in the tower that night Katrine would have to be warned.

As she helped to make the beds she asked her mother, "What do you think of them, Mummy?"

"Well, they are all right, dear. The man seems very friendly. Of course there is no family likeness, but in cousins that is to be expected."

"I suppose they are Katrine's only relations," Mary said thoughtfully.

"Yes, poor child. Still, they mean well by looking her up like this, I'm sure."

Mary said no more. It was just like Mother who always thought the best of everyone.

CHAPTER TWELVE

THE BEARDED MAN

THE TWO boys enjoyed their ride to Glenavar, although the latter part of it was a climb which brought them to the summit of a hill. Glenavar lay below, a large village lying in the glen in the shadow of the mountain.

They stopped at a large inn for a drink of lemonade and to ask directions. Mr. Besant's house lay, they were told, just outside the village, and they pushed on to find it. It was a small, four-square place, most neatly kept, in a really beautiful garden on the verge of a forest of pines which fringed the mountain.

"Mountain! It isn't a mountain," said Andrew. "They aren't really mountains in Scotland."

"You just say that to a Scot and see what he says," laughed Jim, as they propped their machines inside the gate.

"I hope he's in." Andrew stared at the house, then paused to stroke a large, somnolent tabby who lay in the sun by the whitened doorstep.

"He is, there's his car." Jim indicated Mr. Besant's car, which stood by the new-looking garage to one side of the house.

They had scarcely spoken when the door opened and Ronald Besant stood there looking at them in some surprise.

"Hallo," he said, "this is an unexpected pleasure." He gave Jim an anxious glance, "Katrine all right?"

"Why, yes, sir. She's with us again now."

Ronald Besant showed them into a sitting-room.

"That unexpected guest of yours went. She told me that."

"Yes, it's quite O.K. now."

"Well, sit down, and I'll get my housekeeper to bring some refreshments." He looked at them doubtfully and went out. He was away some time, then returned, followed by a tall plain woman who carried a tray laden with glasses, freshly-made orangeade, and a plate of home-made cakes which at once interested Andrew.

The woman smiled at them, then left. Ronald Besant poured out drinks and looked at Jim.

"Now, you came for a purpose. What's the trouble?"

"Katrine didn't tell you about going in the tower yesterday?"

"No, she didn't." The answer was abrupt.

"Oh, it's quite all right, but she found a clue."

Jim went on to tell about Andrew's trespass in the tower, how the two girls had gone down, what they had seen there, and the finding of the golden medallion.

Ronald Besant listened without interrupting, then when Jim had finished he said, "Anything else?"

"Yes, I saw a light in the tower on Friday night, and I waited to see who was there, and saw a man coming out."

The older man still waited.

"And of course there was that other man, a policeman in the grounds . . ."

Besant ignored the second piece of information.

"The man in the tower, you saw him? Can you describe him?"

Jim did the best he could.

"And my young brother saw a man who seems to have been like him, at least he was bald, talking to the Canning character."

"Canning? The man who followed Katrine, you mean?"

"Yes."

"You're sure of that?"

"He was bald and thick-set," interrupted Andrew. "You see, Canning seemed to be waiting in the road, so I watched. This car drove up and stopped, and the bald man got out. Of course we can't be sure he was the same one because Jim didn't see him then."

Mr. Besant seemed to be about to say something when his housekeeper entered and beckoned him outside. He went out, leaving them.

"No wonder Katrine said he was cagey," remarked Andrew.

"Cagey he is, and worried sick about something," agreed Jim.

Besant returned at that moment.

"I'd like a word with you, Jim," he said.

Jim followed him into the hall.

The older man spoke quickly. "Now, Jim, I'm going to trust you. As everyone realises there was something very strange behind the disappearance of the Maclure. MacShane, a C.I.D. man, has been working on it. I think you saw him watching the castle the other night."

"Yes, and Mary has met him."

"Well, as you may have heard, he was shot. We think that perhaps he had found out a little too much. Now a lot depends on how we act now in order to apprehend the criminals behind all this."

"Criminals, sir?" Jim's eyes widened.

"Undoubtedly. A friend of mine is staying with me now. He has been ill, but, well, he knows a good deal. Still he should be kept quiet. Unfortunately, he heard your arrival and asked Biddy about you. Now he insists on seeing you."

"But I don't understand. Why does he want to see me?"

"Never mind that. But come up with me, don't say anything about what you have told me. He's a sick man and mustn't be excited. All I want you to do is reassure him."

Unable to hide his bewilderment, Jim followed Mr. Besant up to a bright sunny room. In a bed by the window lay a large, broad-shouldered man with a grey-flecked dark beard, under it his face looked pale and wasted, but the bright blue eyes were alert enough.

"Hallo," was his greeting, "you're one of the Carew boys Biddy has been telling me about. Katrine is with you now?"

"Yes, sir."

"Is she all right?"

"She's fine, sir."

"She's at the Manse now?"

"Yes."

"Good," he stirred uneasily, "keep an eye on her, tell her to be careful of strangers, any strangers—this is really important."

"I think I understand."

"You don't, but never mind."

Jim was looking a question.

"Well, what is it?"

"I was thinking, sir, about the odd things that have happened, a whole lot of them. Do the police know? They're still investigating."

"I know that, and I think that now they have at last something to go on. But there has to be proof before arresting a criminal you know, lad, proof!"

The voice had become agitated and a flush had risen on the pale face. Besant touched Jim's arm.

"Come now," he said in low tones.

The man in the bed smiled. "It's O.K., Ronald. Jim's

a sensible lad, I can see that. Remember what I said, Jim?"

"Yes, sir."

"See Katrine and tell her not to worry, that she has friends and that all will come right in the end."

"All right, I will." Jim left feeling more bewildered than ever.

Downstairs Andrew was still eating cakes with his usual good appetite.

Ronald Besant saw them out, and as he watched them collect their bicycles, he said, "It won't be long now, I mean all this mystery and anxiety. Remember me to Katrine and tell her about this interview, everything." He gave Jim a long look, seemed about to say more, then left the house.

They cycled through the town in silence. Jim had a lot to think about, but he was glad that he had come over to visit the factor. Ronald Besant definitely knew a great deal of what had been going on and, although he had still been anxious, there had been something in his manner which inferred that, as the stranger had said, all would come out right in the end. He told his brother about his interview with the sick man.

"Rum," was Andrew's comment, "who was he anyway?"

"I don't know—though . . ." Jim broke off. "Let's get on, Andy, it's nearly seven."

Bent over their machines they raced on and back to the Manse.

Meanwhile Mary awaited her brothers' return impatiently. The Maclures had been shown their room and, as far as she could guess, for she had not talked to her alone, Katrine seemed to have accepted them without question.

The house, now really a guest-house with four people to cater for, had to be run, dinner to be prepared. Mary did her various tasks mechanically, waiting for a chance to have a word with her friend alone. She had laid the tables in the dining-room when Katrine came in.

"Well," were her first words, "what do you think of them?" She held out her arm, "Look what Cousin Myra gave me."

On her arm was a beautiful, heavily-carved silver bracelet set with turquoises.

"Nice! What do you think of them, Katrine?"

"They're all right. Cousin Ian seems a good sort. Fancy, they came over when they heard of Father's going like that." She sighed, "I suppose it's something to have someone belonging to one."

Poor Katrine! "I know, I'm glad for you." If Mary sounded doubtful, her friend did not notice.

"And he's given me new hope. Ian Maclure, I mean. He thinks Father may have lost his memory and may still be found."

"That would be wonderful."

"I know. After all he was wounded in Italy. He had head injuries and was unconscious for ages, I do know that."

"I didn't know, but surely that was a long time ago before you were born?"

"Yes." Katrine turned the bracelet round on her arm, and suddenly her eyes filled with tears. "But don't you see, it may be true? Now you're making me doubt it all. Perhaps he was only being kind."

Mary put her arm round the slim shoulders.

"Darling, I'm being horrible. Of course there's hope, after all it's barely a month since he disappeared."

"Yes, a month now. It isn't a very long time, not really."

Mary hesitated. With Katrine in her present mood it would be cruel to mention her suspicions, yet she felt she must.

"What is it?"

"I've got to tell you. Those were the people whom Andrew saw talking to Canning. I rang up about it, didn't Jim tell you?"

"Yes, he did." Katrine laughed. "As a matter of fact Cousin Ian explained that. Think of it, they passed here yesterday and stopped to ask a man for The Old Manse and he told them it was right on the other side of Glenavar. He wilfully misdirected them and they motored on, couldn't find it of course, and as it was by then getting so late, they put up at a hotel on the other side of the glen. So you see."

Mary was relieved. "So that was what they were talking about," she said, "all the same . . ."

"All the same, what?"

"Nothing." It was no use distressing Katrine further, by telling her that even now, until Jim saw him, she was not sure that the man who had been in the tower by night was the same man as this Maclure who had come to-day.

Katrine was staring at her curiously when someone called from the hall.

"Katrine—Katrine, my dear."

It was Ian Maclure, looking very spruce in well-cut tweeds and a fresh shirt, his balding head shining.

He smiled at them both, his full moon-like face the picture of amiability.

"Ah, there you are, and our dear Mary who has been such a good friend to you. Your Cousin Myra is titivating—suppose you show me the grounds of this delectable place?"

Katrine went out with him willingly enough, and Mary went on with her chores very thoughtfully.

It was nearly half past six. If only the boys would return! She wished they had never gone over to Glenavar, for once Jim saw the man Maclure he would surely know whether it *had* been he creeping from the tower room.

She returned to the kitchen and was creaming potatoes for Lilian, when Katrine came bursting in.

She spoke to Mary's mother, "I say, what time is dinner?"

"Half past seven, dear. Why?"

"Well, my cousins thought we could run over to the castle. Cousin Ian has a theory he wants to test. He seems to know something—though he won't tell me what it is yet. Anyhow they're terribly keen to see the castle."

"If you like I can put off your dinner until eight, dear."

"Would you? We shan't be long. I'll just show them round a bit, and we're taking the car."

Mary spoke quickly. "Katrine, don't go."

"Why ever not?"

"Look, the boys will be back soon. Please don't go!"

"Give me one good reason why I shouldn't. It's a lovely evening, and we shall skirt the loch. It's five miles by road, but in that car we shall do it in a quarter of an hour—or less." She smiled at them all. "Be seeing you," and turned away.

Mary ran after her and caught her up in the hall.

"Katrine, *please* don't go."

"Really, Mary, I don't know what's come over you. I know you hate me to be alone in the castle, but I shan't be alone."

"Wait until Jim gets back—he can't be long now."

A thick-set figure appeared from the lounge. Ian

Maclure held a panama under his arm, and his wife was behind him teetering on her very high heels.

"Ah, there you are. Now come along, you're our guide, remember."

Katrine picked up a head-scarf from the hall table and patted Mary's arm.

"Coming. We'll be back in a hour, sweetie."

Helplessly Mary watched them go out and get into the car. Mechanically she rescued Boodle, who had been exploring under it, and stood, the cat in her arms, watching the car turn and drive away.

The colonel crossed the hall, book under arm.

"Anything wrong, my dear?" he asked, noticing her troubled face.

Mary forced a smile. "No, no, of course not."

It didn't help that her mother and Lilian commented on Katrine's happy reaction to her cousins' arrival; it didn't help at all. Mary was afraid, and afraid for Katrine.

That stout, round-faced man was too amiable, too effusive. Surely Katrine saw that? But no, he had given her hope and that had meant all the world to her.

The boys turned up about a quarter of an hour after Katrine's departure with her cousins.

Mary hurried round to the shed where they were putting away their bicycles.

"What's the matter?" asked Jim at once.

"Katrine's cousins from New Zealand have come. They were the people we saw, Andrew and me, talking to the Canning man yesterday."

Jim stiffened. "Oh, gosh, I wish I'd seen them. Where are they now?"

Mary shook her head as she answered, "They've gone to the castle."

"Good life, she's gone with them alone?"

"Yes, by car. They left about a quarter of an hour ago."

"But you should have stopped her!"

"I tried. The man explained about talking to Canning. He said Canning misdirected them when they were looking for us. It—it may be all right. . . ."

"Maybe is the word. Of course it *could* be quite all right. If only I knew whether he was the man I saw in the tower."

He turned to the house. "Which is their room?"

"Why?"

"They've unpacked, I suppose—there may be some clue."

The Maclures had been given one of the larger rooms over the garden. Mrs. Maclure had unpacked, and toilet articles lay on the old-fashioned dressing table and on the wash-stand. On the table by the window were some books and papers.

Jim went straight to these and turned them over.

"Nothing here—guide-books, letters directed to the Hamilton Hotel, London. Name's Maclure all right."

Mary went over to the dressing-table and picked up a small leather-bound article. It was the kind of photograph container one can carry about. She opened it. There were two photographs in it, one of Mrs. Maclure, her hair elaborately waved, and one of Ian Maclure, his usual amiable grin showing under his balding head.

"Look." She handed it to Jim.

Jim looked, and his face was set.

"Mary, this *is* the man, I'm all but certain it is. It's the man I saw coming out of the tower."

They looked at each other in growing apprehension. Andrew who had been moving restlessly round the room, came up. "What's that, a photograph?"

Both ignored him. Jim ran out and down the stairs two at a time.

"What are you going to do?" Mary called after him.

"I'm going to contact Besant. He may be able to do something."

"But what? Shouldn't you get the police?"

"What could I tell them? Anyway, MacShane must still be in hospital. No, Besant is the one, and the bearded man."

"The bearded man . . .?"

"Yes, he was at Besant's house. He's been ill, pretty bad I'd say, but he insisted on seeing me and asking about Katrine."

"But, Jim . . ."

Jim had no time for further explanations. He hurried into the hall to telephone. He got through to the factor at once and Mary heard him relate the cousins' arrival succinctly, and how he suspected, that the man was the one he had seen coming from the tower. Then he waited for instructions which came quickly enough.

He looked puzzled. "Go over at once? Yes, but who could we take? There's Colonel Brayne . . . he'll do? As a witness? . . . What does it all mean, sir?"

Evidently Ronald Besant did not explain further, for Jim put down the receiver, his face still anxious.

"We've got to follow Katrine to the castle at once. Besant's joining us there. He said to take someone reliable with us, and I could only think of the colonel."

"We'll go across the loch?"

"Yes, Murdo can row us over, we could take him up to the castle too, he's pretty hefty."

He rushed out, and Mary and Andrew followed.

"I'd rather you didn't come," he said over his shoulder.

"I'm coming," Mary told him firmly.

"And me," added Andrew.

"Where's the colonel? I must ask him to come." Jim went on.

"Over there in the garden," she said with a quick nod.

Jim approached him. What he said Mary did not hear, but it must have satisfied the older man for he went straight into the hall to get his coat.

"Run and tell Mother to wait dinner for us," said Jim.

Mary ran, literally, in case they did go without her, confronted her bewildered mother in the kitchen, and said, as calmly as she could, "Mum, we've got to go to the castle. We shan't be long but can you keep dinner until eightish?"

"To the castle? But why? Are you joining Katrine and her cousins?"

Andrew, who had followed his sister, looked longingly at the fruit salads waiting on the table.

"It's a matter of life and death," he pronounced solemnly.

As they hurried out Mary only hoped that he was not speaking the truth.

CHAPTER THIRTEEN

THE SECRET OF THE CASTLE

WHEN MARY looked back on that hurried return to the castle and on what happened there, her recollections were to remain with her like bad dreams verging on nightmares. Like all dreams, of course, it ended, though not so soon as she would have wished.

When she and Andrew left the Manse they found that Jim was already at the landing-stage with the colonel.

He turned irritably. "Look here, Mary, you and Andrew will only be in the way."

"I must come. Really, Jim, Katrine may need me."

Rather to her surprise the colonel interposed. "Surely the more the merrier. They'll be all right with us, Jim."

So Jim had not told him a great deal; after all there had not been time.

For once Murdo was nowhere about, but the boat they used swung gently at its moorings, and Jim sprang in and took up the oars.

As the colonel followed he said, "Some of these old places are danger traps. But surely your friend, Katrine, is it, will not venture into this tower you tell me of?"

Jim helped Mary down and Andrew followed quickly. Mary sat next to Colonel Brayne and took the ropes.

"As a matter of fact, sir," said Jim, "there's a great deal more to it than an ordinary dangerous building. We'll tell you later, if you don't mind."

The loch was still choppy and high—there had been heavy rains in the mountains and the burns that fed it affected the swell.

As they veered out, Mary suddenly remembered the doggerel verse.

> "*If loch be high,*
>   *There's greetin' nigh,*
> *Tak nae step doon*
> *Frae nicht tae noon.*"

She quoted it slowly and Jim nodded. "Scrawled on that door, you say?"

"I was wondering why. Jim, there is something rather frightening about that tower. Who could have written that though?"

"From what Andrew told me it must have been a place where prisoners were kept; perhaps some poor creature scrawled it there."

"Do you think Katrine will take them down there?"

"That's what I'm afraid of. Remember how we said we wouldn't explore it without some adult with us. And she doesn't know what we know."

"Ronald is coming?"

"Oh, yes, it'll take him a bit of time by road but he'll come."

The colonel listened shrewdly but made no remark. No doubt he thought he was being taken on a wild goose chase, but he merely glanced at them with a kind of amused interest.

When they reached the landing-stage and scrambled out, it was Mary who led the way round to the front of the castle. The sun on its lines of windows was reflected redly, for the sun that evening was descending slowly in a riot of colour.

There was no sign of anyone in the grounds, the place itself seemed absolutely deserted, then, as they turned round to the back, there stood the Maclures' Daimler.

"I expect Katrine took them in by the back," said Jim.

It was true; the door to the kitchen quarters which they had used was open.

"They're still here anyway," the colonel spoke consolingly.

Mary was already hurrying along the passage. She led the way to the great main hall and, once there, they all stood listening.

The colonel raised his voice.

"Anyone about?" he called in a parade voice.

There was no answer, but Mary thought she heard steps above. "Upstairs," she said.

They raced up the wide staircase, hesitated and then a voice called, "Hallo there, is that you, Katrine?"

"The gallery," hissed Jim.

Down the wide corridor they went, Jim pushed wide the doors and there, staring at the lines of pictures in the light from the golden sun which now streamed through the windows, were the two people who called themselves Katrine's cousins.

The man advanced, head forward in a way he had. Andrew who had been following them in silence, whispered, "It *is* the man I saw in the car."

Jim did not need to be told this—he had almost recoiled, for the stance as well as the bald head were familiar.

Meanwhile the man was speaking.

"Hallo! Quite a party. Seen anything of Katrine? She was showing us these most interesting portraits when suddenly we missed her. She just seemed to vanish."

"And we were going up to the tower. The view from the top must be wonderful," lamented his wife.

"What have you done with her?" asked Jim harshly.

"Done with her? My dear boy, what on earth do you mean?"

Jim faced him. "Well, what were you doing here on Sunday night? I saw you come from the tower. I think you've got a lot to explain, sir."

The colonel broke in suavely.

"These young people have been warned about some danger to do with this place—in the tower, I gather. Have you been there?"

The bald man looked very bland, but his eyes were watchful.

"I told you we haven't," said the woman. "Katrine just walked out on us."

Jim turned. "Come on, Mary. Colonel, will you come with us?"

"Of course." He turned. "I shouldn't worry, this seems to be an immense place, easy to disappear for a while in it."

Mrs. Maclure hesitated, and lingered by a portrait between the windows—that of a fair, stoutish man painted in the late seventeenth century.

"We had just discovered this, and remarked on the likeness when she left us," she remarked.

Mary gave a cursory glance at the portrait, then it held her attention, although Jim was already leading the way out.

The round face, the light eyes under thinning fair hair, held a remarkable likeness to the thick-set man now moving away with the others. Whatever lay behind it all, he was a Maclure after all, as the portrait showed.

She moved ahead and caught up with Jim and Andrew.

"Where are you going?" she asked.

"To the tower of course."

"Do you think then . . .?"

"Never mind what I think. Katrine's disappeared, hasn't she? We're going to look into the place."

Along those eternal passages, up and down steps and finally, the door loomed beyond its heavy curtain.

Jim pushed it wide and looked back grimly, watching the two Maclures following somewhat doubtfully.

The colonel entered and glanced about him with interest.

"By jove, this must date back some hundreds of years," he said.

Andrew was already clattering down the first set of stairs, but the others followed more cautiously. A glance round the first room showed nothing—it was as they had left it, Mary realised, when Andrew had trespassed before.

"What about the turret?" she asked Jim in low tones. "No, it's down here we must look over first."

Mr. Maclure's thick, rather plaintive, voice remarked, "Most interesting, but surely Katrine would not venture here alone?"

"Not alone." Jim gave him a hard glance which the other returned in a kind of bland reproach.

Down again and into the Room of the Mirror. There were exclamations, and the colonel at once examined the bronze.

"Surely we need go no farther," said Mrs. Maclure unhappily.

"You can stay up here if you like," said Jim, "I'm going down."

He struggled with the door of the mirror, then the colonel leaned over and did something to the heavy latch. It moved out easily. "Odd that," he said, half to himself, "been oiled lately."

Everyone, everyone, that is, except Jim and the colonel, hesitated, as the door revealed more winding steps, slimy with damp, and dripping walls. It was quite dark.

It was Maclure who took out a small torch from his

pocket and cast the light before him, showing them the way.

The torch he had used the other night?

Jim went down doggedly. But Mary hesitated. What would they find below? What secret did this dreadful place hide?

"Come on," said Andrew. "We're not alone now." She came, but reluctantly.

One turn, two, then suddenly it was as though the loch was all around them by the sound and the smell.

"Back!" shouted the colonel, only just in time. The comparatively faint light of the torch revealed, not a solid floor, but a moving mass of water.

They all stood on the stairs, staring down. Maclure cast his light round.

The four dripping walls were evil-smelling, with slimy creatures adhering to them. In the walls were three iron rings and, as in the room above, broken chains.

The waters of the loch were coming in by some scarcely discernable sluice-gate deep on the fourth wall, coming and rising.

If loch be high, there's greetin' nigh . . .

"Come back, come out of this horrible place!" wailed Mrs. Maclure from behind them.

"Pass me your torch, please." The colonel turned to the man behind it. He took it and slowly, very carefully, cast the circle of light all over the place.

Whatever he hoped or dreaded to see, was not there: there was only the churning water of the rising loch, nothing more. The water was churning even over the chains and rings in the wall.

"All right. Nothing more to see," he said.

Thankfully they all climbed up the stairs and, once in the comparative dry of the room above, Maclure intoned his verdict.

"My ancestors were a nice lot. Must have put their prisoners down there chained to the wall, waiting for a grisly death by water. Not a nice place."

No one made any reply.

Mrs. Maclure was already negotiating the next stairway. Mary followed with Jim and Andrew.

"Nothing there, Jim."

"I know. Thank goodness."

"But where is Katrine?"

He did not answer.

They moved with relief into the main part of the great place and had reached the main stairs when the jangling of the bell reached them.

Jim ran on ahead. "It will be Besant," he muttered, "though I don't see what good he can do now."

He was unchaining the great door as the others came down and stood in an undecided group in the hall.

Ronald Besant stood there, and, behind him were two men, one an erect military-looking man in tweeds, and, leaning on a stick, still pale and apparently weak after his mysterious illness, the bearded man Jim had seen only that afternoon.

It was he who spoke first, hustling forward into the hall.

"Where's Katrine?"

"We don't know. But she isn't in the tower, we looked," piped up Andrew. Then he stopped.

Everyone was staring at the bald, thick-set figure of Ian Maclure who had been standing with them when the door was opened.

Now, when the bearded man moved forward he took a step back. Mary stared at him: there was an unhealthy pallor on his round face, and he put his hand to his throat as though terrified, then turned as though ready for flight.

His wife caught his arm. "What is it, Ian? Do you feel unwell?"

The bearded man now confronted him.

"So you recognise me, eh? Surprised, eh?"

But the other did not wait to reply. He turned and ran out of the hall and away up one of the many passages.

They all stared after him. The military man shrugged. "I've got some men outside, he won't get away," he said.

The bearded man did not seem to hear. He turned to Jim.

"I want to know about Katrine. Where is she?" he repeated almost incoherently.

"When we arrived the Maclures said she had been with them, then vanished," was all the boy could say.

"Vanished?" The face was very pale, the eyes overbright. "Have you searched the tower?"

"Yes, we've all been down, right down."

"To the loch room, the trap?"

"Yes, yes."

He turned to the woman who stood staring numbly down the passage as though expecting her husband to return.

"You're Ian's wife?"

"Yes."

"If anything has happened to Katrine, you'd better tell me."

She shivered, her faded eyes frightened. "We were in the gallery and she was showing us the portraits. Then suddenly she wasn't there, she'd just left us. She was going to take us to the tower, my husband had asked her, but . . ."

He turned away. "We'll have to search the place."

Mary was thinking more coherently now. Suppose Katrine, unsuspecting, had been showing them the pictures and then something had happened to frighten her. The most sensible thing to do would be to run away without arousing their own suspicions. So far so good. She would leave her cousins busy looking at the portraits. Where would she go? Return to the Manse or stay somewhere in the castle until the coast was clear? She knew it well, naturally enough, and there were rooms, large and small in which she could hide. Hide?

Abruptly Mary turned and made her way quietly up the stairs, leaving the little group of people, including Jim and Andrew, already organising a search in the hall. She found her way along a now familiar corridor to the two rooms they had occupied, the Oriel rooms. She tried the door. It was locked.

"Katrine?" she called.

No answer, then, "Mary! Mary, is that you?"

"Of course. Let me in. It's all right. Everyone's here, Mr. Besant and a high-ranking policeman of some sort, and a bearded man I've never seen before who seems terribly upset about you. And the colonel and us . . ." she was rather incoherent as Katrine opened the door and stood staring at her.

"Mary, this is wonderful. What made you come?"

"Jim saw a photograph of your cousin. He was the man Jim saw the other night coming out of the tower. You must have been in danger, pretty bad danger, but what made you guess and come here?"

Katrine shook her head. "I didn't suspect a thing. They were my cousins—I wasn't madly keen on them, but after all they were of my family. We came here and I showed them round then to the picture gallery. We were going to the tower afterwards, but only up to see the view. They were both keen to do that. Then as I was looking at the pictures with them, I saw the Ian Maclure who betrayed his brother to the Covenanters long ago, and I remembered the old story that in every two generations or so, a White Maclure has evil blood in him. I looked at that man, my cousin, and he was a White Maclure and suddenly, I don't know why, I was afraid. 'Always beware of a White Maclure,' they say. When an albino is born in the family he is evil.''

"And you ran away."

"Yes, I just came here and locked myself in. It was a crazy thing to do, but I did."

Mary laughed a trifle too gaily. "Your feminine intuition, Katrine. Well, he's gone anyway. He saw Mr. Besant and the other man and the bearded man and just ran for it."

"But why? He hadn't done anything."

"I've no idea why. But do come down—they're all worried sick about you."

"I'm glad Ronald's come, I've got to talk with him." The old look of worry was on her face again, and Mary remembered.

"And Katrine, we've been in the tower, right down to the lowest chamber."

Katrine stopped. "What was there?" she asked sharply.

"Nothing at all. Only water. When the loch is high the water comes right up and into the room. It was used to trap prisoners in the bad old days."

"You're sure? Nothing else?"

"Absolutely nothing."

From the sound of voices the other visitors had moved into one of the big lounges off the hall.

Arm in arm, Katrine and Mary went in.

They were all there, the boys, the men, and Mrs. Maclure, the latter sitting by the window, tense and unhappy.

"Look who's here!" cried Mary.

The men turned. Jim said something which sounded like "Thank heavens for that," and Andrew dashed up to them.   Suddenly Mary felt the arm holding hers go stiff, and saw that the bearded man was coming towards them.

"My dear," he began.

He got no further, for Katrine's arm went limp and, before Mary could steady her, she had fallen to the floor in a dead faint.

CHAPTER FOURTEEN

ALL RIGHT IN THE END

It was Ronald Besant who lifted Katrine gently and laid her, a cushion under her head, on one of the settees.

The bearded man leaned over her and took her hand in his. "It's all right, my dear. All right," he murmured.

Practical as ever, Jim rushed off for water, but, by the time he had come back, Katrine had opened her eyes. Mary, who stood by her, saw her look at the bearded man. Then she spoke weakly, "I think I knew all the time. You just couldn't be dead, Father," she said.

"No, but I've only been in my right mind for the last three days. I had a crack on the head. It affected my old injury, and I lost my memory."

She sat up, colour returning.

"Mary, this is my father. You see, I was right to come here after all."

Ronald Besant shook his head. "I'm not so sure of that. A good thing you got away just now."

"From my cousins? But they wouldn't have dared do anything to me!"

She stared round the room. The fair woman, who was Ian Maclure's wife, was looking at her in a kind of desperation.

"Where is Ian Maclure?" she asked.

Her father smiled grimly. "He saw me, must have thought I was a ghost, and ran for it. The Chief Inspector who came with us, had the place surrounded. He's gone off now to see if he has been caught."

"I wish I understood." She caught her father's hand

and held it close. "Anyhow you're back. Daddy, you *do* look ill. You are all right?"

He smiled. "Nothing wrong with me that a few days' rest won't cure."

Mary moved away and gave Jim and Andrew a meaning look. "I'm going to make some tea," she said. "I know we could all do with some. Come on, you two."

"A very good idea," Alan Maclure, the Maclure, agreed. "I'm grateful to you young people for all your help. I don't know what Katrine would have done without you."

"I hope you'll tell us all about it, sir," said Jim.

"Suppose you get that cup of tea first."

The colonel had gone off to look round the castle, the chief inspector had not yet returned, and as the Carews went out, Mary glimpsed Mrs. Maclure moving almost unsteadily to the hall. She felt sorry for her. Whatever her husband had planned she had known nothing of it.

As they went up to the room to use the oil-stove Mary's mind was churning with questions.

"But what happened to him—the Maclure, I mean," she asked, as she found some tea left among the provisions in the room. "It was so tough on Katrine."

Andrew had found some biscuits.

"That's what I'd like to know."

"He had amnesia, didn't you hear him tell Katrine?" said Jim.

"What's amnesia?" From Andrew, of course.

"Loss of memory. Let's get this tea, then perhaps he'll talk."

It took some little time, as there was not enough china and Mary had to go into the big kitchen, find a tray and assemble cups and saucers there. Finally, with Jim carrying the tray, they returned to the sitting-room.

Katrine was sitting up watching her father, who had

found a chair near her, as though she expected him to vanish into thin air again.   Ronald Besant and the colonel were smoking and talking, and there was no sign of Mrs. Maclure.   It turned out later that she had left the castle alone and the police had not detained her, knowing that she would, sooner or later, contact her husband who was already in custody.

Mary poured out the tea, whilst Jim went into the hall to ring up the Manse and tell their mother that they would be delayed for some time yet.

And it was over the tea that the Maclure told them his story.

"It was in the middle of July," he began, "that I got a letter from Ian Maclure telling me that he and his wife were in England.   I was alone here apart from the servants, though I expected guests later in the month. Well, they were relations, the only ones we had, so I asked them over.   I had no reply, then one evening, it was a Tuesday of the next week, I remember, Ian drove up alone.   He had left his wife in London, he said.   Naturally I asked him to stay."   He paused, frowning.   "Can't say I took to him from the first.   There was something too effusive about him, too—well, smarmy, and as soon as I saw him, I realised that he was one of the 'White Maclures' as we have always called them.   Whether by chance or not I can't say, but the 'White Maclures' who seem to be born into the family now and then, have always been a shifty lot and worse.   Still he had come, and White Maclure or not, I had to entertain him."

He stopped and smiled reassuringly at his daughter. "The loch was high at that time after a series of storms, but when he suggested I show him the tower, I did so without suspecting any ill-intention on his part.   His request came that evening after dinner.   We had been talking of the legend, and I had explained that the place had been a kind of 'oubliette,' a trap for the unwary, in the bad old days. He was interested. Now I should add that as I had been going south that week before my guests arrived, to attend a dinner of my old regiment, I had let my housekeeper and batman go off for a holiday. A cold meal had been left by the daily servants who had not seen Ian Maclure. Consequently, when they were questioned, they knew nothing of him. To continue. We went to the tower. I had no intention of going down to the lower chambers, especially the lowest of all which would be a death trap, but, talking excitedly, Ian went on ahead, then, in spite of my warning, opened the Mirror Door and ventured down." He stopped. "The rest is vague in my mind. I think I heard him slip, and call for help. I went after him and he struck out at me. I stumbled and fell—being taken entirely by surprise—and a moment later I was in the water. I had fallen heavily on those steps and practically stunned myself, but the sudden immersion helped, for I began to swim for my life. I managed to regain the steps and crawled up them, only to find that the door had been slammed on me. I was trapped. The iron gratings of the sluice gates there were broken and I forced myself out and into the loch. I swam ashore, scrambled on to a bank and lost consciousness."

Katrine had gone very white. He patted her hand. "Don't look so distressed, my dear. I'm all right, as you see."

"But why didn't you get help, sir?" asked Jim.

He shook his head.

"When I came to myself I couldn't remember a thing. I had been struck on the head, remember, and it had affected an old war injury. I got up and wandered off, unable to remember my identity or what I was doing there. For a while I thought I was in Italy and that

I must get away—my old experiences returning. I had to get away, that seemed the most important thing. I stumbled on through the wild country beyond the park—I must have gone north." He put his hand to his head, "Even now I cannot recollect how far I wandered or even where. Only I must have lost consciousness again for, when I came to, I was in a shepherd's hut. My head had been roughly bandaged, and the shepherd himself, an old man, tended me. The place was isolated and there was nothing on me to show my identity as such papers as had been in my pockets had been ruined by water. Old Tammas, I seem to remember that was his name, was something of a hermit. He kept telling me that he would take me into the town as soon as I was well enough to move, but he never saw a newspaper and he accepted my presence philosophically, much as he would have a sick sheep, and did his considerable best for me.

"Anyhow he was busy with his sheep and I must have been an anxiety to him. How long I was there I do not know. Finally old Tammas got a doctor to me. The doctor was a busy man, and with my torn clothes and rough beard I must have seemed little but a vagrant, but he ordered an ambulance to take me to hospital at Perth. Once there I began to remember, and my first thoughts were for Katrine. I asked the date and was worried sick when I found that I had been lost for three weeks. Katrine would know I had disappeared. Was she safe in London? Would that evil cousin of mine get in touch with her? I had to get away. I was afraid and furiously angry. So I said nothing to the people in the hospital that first day, pretending that my memory had not returned. That night I got my clothes out of the locker and slipped away. It took me some time to reach Glenavar. Bearded, shabby, I all but begged my way south, my one intention to get to the castle and in touch with Ronald here." He smiled at his factor, "You didn't know me at first, did you, Ronald?"

Besant shook his head ruefully, "I heard from the police that an unknown man who might be you had been traced to the hospital. The police arrived the morning after you went, having been diverted from their search in the district. You should have trusted them, Maclure."

The big man put his hand to his head wearily. "I know, I know, I suppose I was still a bit off my head. Two things seemed most important: to get back to Lendaloch and find what had happened, and then contact Katrine."

"Why didn't you send for me at once?" asked Katrine.

He smiled, "It was only the matter of a day. You were apparently safe. I got in touch with the police from Ronald's and they decided to lay a trap for the villain of the piece who had been seen in the district with a man very well known to Scotland Yard. As you may have heard I saw young Jim Carew. I wasn't to know that my dear cousin had acted so quickly and had actually arrived at the Manse."

Katrine shivered unconsciously.

"I never suspected them of course, any more than you did. When they suggested a drive to the castle it seemed reasonable enough." She paused, "I should say ' he,' poor cousin Myra doesn't know a thing about the plot, I'm sure of that."

There was a short silence.

"To think that it was he I saw in the tower the other night," said Jim.

Katrine's father nodded, "Setting his trap, no doubt. He knew Katrine had come to Lendaloch, and he knew she suspected Canning. What better way than to send Canning to the Manse and scare her away to the very place where she would be in danger?"

"Exactly what I did." Katrine smiled. "Luckily we didn't really know how bad the danger was. Still "—she smiled at the Carews—"I had fine guards all the time."

The Maclure smiled at Mary. "Yes, I've a lot to thank you young people for. Of course Cousin Ian overplayed his hand when he shot at MacShane in the grounds. That only substantiated my story to the police. After that he must have returned to Perth which he had made his headquarters, got in touch with his accomplice Canning, then arrived at the Manse."

"Did you say Canning is a crook?" asked Jim.

"Yes, that's true. He is a man ready to do any dirty work for a price. This particular work was to keep an eye on Katrine, and, as I told you, to scare her from the Manse and if possible to the castle. I was frantic when I heard that she had been there and might return. In my desire for revenge, I felt, I had, like Ian Maclure, overplayed my hand, and not trusted the police sufficiently."

"The plot was to get Katrine out of the way?" said Mary faintly.

"Yes," he agreed, grimly. "With Katrine and me both dead, nothing stood between Ian Maclure and Lendaloch. He was the only heir, and the stake was high."

"That was why he left the door to the tower open then?" said Jim. "Good thing we didn't venture."

"Yes, he hoped she would fall into the trap. She had always been curious about the place, for the simple reason that it was forbidden territory."

"And they were going to do something like that to-day?" Jim asked.

The Maclure nodded soberly: "A fall from the tower, a slip in the water below, either would have served."

"And that dreadful man has got away?" Mary felt a little sick.

The Maclure shook his head. "Oh, no. The police know the whole story now. And it so happens that he is wanted for robbery with violence in New Zealand."

The shadows were gathering. Mary looked round the large and beautiful room with a feeling of unreality.

The Maclure got up, swaying a little, and Ronald took his arm. "Time you got back to bed, sir."

The other smiled. "Time we all made tracks. Katrine, you go back to the Manse, my dear."

The little party split up rather silently. All were thinking of the terrible story they had heard.

It was Ronald who drove them to the Manse, for neither Katrine, nor Mary and her brothers, fancied the shorter row across the loch in the growing darkness.

Once at the Manse, Katrine clung to her father for a moment.

"I hope I'm forgiven," he said, "for all your anxiety."

"What else could you do, Daddy? But please, get that horrid beard off, or Mary will go on calling you ' the man with the beard ' for the rest of her life."

As they entered the hall Mrs. Carew, with one glance at Katrine, said, "What you've all been up to, I've no idea—that can keep—but bed for *you*, my dear."

So to bed Katrine went, although the family sat over their meal and discussed the whole story, with the colonel and his wife interested and almost incredulous listeners.

It was two weeks later that, one sunny afternoon, a car called at the Manse to take them all, with the exception of Lilian who was content to stay and manage the guests, of whom there were now five, to the castle.

The news of the Maclure's return after his disappearance for a whole month had made headlines even in the London papers. But the truth behind it all had not been published. He had been suffering from loss of memory due to an old war wound, was what had been given out, which was certainly true as far as it went.

As for the Ian Maclures, they were both on their way back to New Zealand to stand trial for quite another piece of villainy.

To-day Mary wore a new and pretty frock, her fair hair shone, and even the boys were spruced up, for it was Katrine's seventeenth birthday and the castle was celebrating the occasion with the help of a few friends in the neighbourhood.

Colonel Brayne and his wife sat with Mrs. Carew in the back of the commodious car, with Andrew, Jim and Mary packed with the chauffeur in front. The chauffeur for this occasion was Ferguson who, if he guessed a good deal of what had happened, accepted it with true Scottish phlegm.

At last they drew up by the big drive gates, and waited for the short, grinning Cockney, Tom Nicholson, to open them. Mary drew a breath of sheer happiness as they drove up to the castle itself.

"It looks lovely to-day," she said, not glancing at the tower beyond which held such grim memories.

It did look lovely. The windows shone, the gardens were in their prime, and, on the terrace above the wide stairway to the great door, a few of the guests were to be seen, talking.

The car had scarcely come to a stop when Katrine, wearing a wide dress over a froth of petticoats, hurried up to them.

She hugged Mary, kissed Mrs. Carew, smiled vivaciously at the boys, then led them up to the terrace to be introduced to some of her friends who had come over to congratulate her.

They were talking to some young people—the two

daughters and son of the minister at Glenavar, when a tall, broad man in a kilt came up.

Mary stared at him, for a moment taking him for a stranger, this handsome man wearing the Maclure tartan, with the big-featured, handsome face.

"It's Daddy without the beard," laughed Katrine. "Really he rather fancied it, I believe, but I made him shave it off for to-day."

He paused for a word with them, then took their mother to introduce her to his friends.

Katrine caught Mary and Jim by the arms.

"Come and see everything," she said. "Andrew, there are ices in the buffet!"

Presently the three of them were moving through the rooms, all polished and shining, and all, as Mary put it, "lived in." They paused for a word with stout, pleasant Mrs. O'Reilly, now installed again as housekeeper, then went up to the two rooms which Mary and Katrine remembered so well.

The sitting-room had some new chairs, pretty blue and green curtains and a toning carpet. Books were on the shelves and there was a small transistor set as well as a radiogram there.

"My very own boudoir," announced Katrine grandly. "I asked Father if I could have these rooms for my very own and he said yes, and had them practically refurnished."

"You're lucky," said Jim. "Must feel fine to have all this," he added teasingly.

"It does. And Jim, we may meet in Edinburgh in about a year's time."

"How come?"

"Daddy's letting me study to be a doctor. It will take ages of course, but I'm starting as early as I can."

"Good for you. But I'm not sure we shall meet, much as I'd like it."

Mary gave him a quick glance. "Don't be silly. Of course you can. The Manse is doing fine, being a real success, and Katrine's father has promised to get us as many guests as we can take."

Katrine nodded. "It's true, you know. We sometimes have an overflow here when the children come over, and we're having twenty of the little rascals next week."

Mary stared. "Twenty children?"

"From Glasgow. Oh, they're pickles and need at least four people to keep an eye on them, but it's fun and we love it."

Mary remembered how she had told them that they took poor children here in the summer.

But Katrine was looking at Jim.

"So, you see, you'll go to Edinburgh and perhaps we'll meet at lectures and all that." She waited.

Jim was looking at her, at her dark eyes, and her soft hair now free round her oval face.

"I say," he managed at last, "that would be wonderful!" They smiled at each other, then laughed. Katrine turned away suddenly, her face a little flushed, and began to show them some new records she had bought.

Katrine and Jim, thought Mary, the two people apart from her mother and Andrew, she loved most in the world. It was good to think that they had grown to like each other, that the link with their families would continue even when they were away studying.

She was to remember that moment of a happy day, a very happy day, finishing with a small impromptu dance in the long gallery.

Only Andrew and the Braynes left early, and Lilian came over to join them all.

As Mary danced, not very proficiently yet, with the tall, red-headed boy who was the minister's son, she stared over his shoulder at the lines of portraits, portraits of the Maclures. One, she noticed, was missing, the one of the "White Maclure," which resembled so closely that unpleasant man, Ian Maclure, who had given them so many anxious hours.

But that was all behind them. Before them lay pleasant summer days, busy days at The Old Manse, happy days here, before she and Katrine returned to school.

A great deal had happened, but all had come right in the end.

THE END